HEIR WITH MY ENEMY

JACKIE ASHENDEN

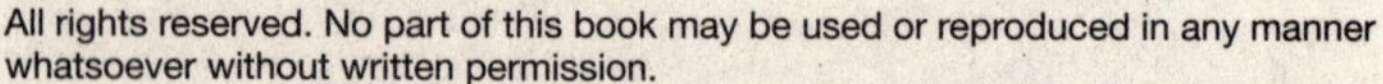

Recycling programs
for this product may
not exist in your area.

ISBN-13: 978-1-335-21390-7

Heir with My Enemy

Harlequin Enterprises ULC
22 Adelaide St. West, 41st Floor
Toronto, Ontario M5H 4E3, Canada
www.Harlequin.com

HarperCollins Publishers
Macken House, 39/40 Mayor Street Upper,
Dublin 1, D01 C9W8, Ireland
www.HarperCollins.com

Printed in Lithuania

1 2 3 4 5 6 7 8 9 10 LIT 28 27 26 25

"Hello?" Beatrix says, answering immediately, and no matter how long it's been since I heard her husky little voice, the effect it has on me is the same.

Every muscle in my body tenses and all I can think about is that same voice begging me in the church as I pushed inside her, *Please...oh please...*

"Miss Morgan," I say, deliberately not using her married name. "It appears we need to have a little chat."

"Santiago," she says eventually, her tone admirably cool. "Or should I say, *Mr. Veracruz*? How nice of you to call. What would you like to chat about?"

Oh, she's good. She's very good. Perfect even, especially with that faint note of surprise at the end. Another person might think she's being genuine, but I know better.

"Come now, Miss Morgan." I turn away from the window and pace over to my desk. "Let's not pretend. I know about your pregnancy."

HEIR WITH MY ENEMY

To the inimitable Caitlin Crews
and to sitting around tables, plotting books. :-)

PROLOGUE

Santiago

I'M STANDING AT the bar at another fundraiser, this time in the Turbine Hall of the Tate Modern. The place is packed with captains of industry, politicians, and other varieties of rich and famous, and I'm rapidly losing patience with the endless list of social events on my calendar.

This gala is to raise money for more computers in schools—a worthy cause—and it's aimed at the tech industry. So, as the CEO of VZ Industries, a very successful research and development company, I should find this a prime hunting ground for more investors.

Yet I'm bored, and restless, and I'm tired of being here already. I don't do small talk, and so I've run out of my meagre store of conversation already, and it's only been half an hour. There are people waiting to talk to me—I can see them considering approaching out of the corner of my eye—but I'm done for the evening, and, having already made a large donation to the cause, I can see no benefit from staying any longer.

And then I see her.

She's standing down the other end of the bar, a wealth of glorious blonde hair cascading over her shoulders, wearing a strapless gown of rose-coloured silk. Her face is picture-perfect beautiful, with arched golden brows, a determined little chin, and a rosebud of a mouth. She's waiting for her drink, and she looks nervous, fingers moving restlessly on the clutch bag that matches her gown. The barman pushes a flute of champagne in her direction and she grabs at it, lifting it to that perfect mouth and taking a little sip.

She must have felt me staring, because that's when her thick, silky lashes lift and eyes of deep midnight-blue meet mine, and a current of electricity abruptly charges the space between us. It's instant and hot, and I know from the way her eyes widen that I'm not alone in feeling it, that she feels it too.

There's a moment when we stare at each other, and everyone else at this pointless gala disappears. It's only her and me at the bar, caught in this intense pull of attraction that neither of us can break.

Colour sweeps across her lovely face, and before I can think better of it I'm moving towards her. It feels as if she is the most beautiful and fascinating thing I've ever seen, though logically I've seen—and had—plenty of other beautiful and fascinating women before. Except she is different and I'm not sure why. This attraction is a force of nature, elemental almost, and I've certainly never felt it this intensely before.

Her colour deepens as I approach, her gaze locked with mine, and her mouth begins to curl as I get closer.

It's welcome I see in those lovely blue eyes, as well as an acknowledgement of the need that gets more intense as I stop right beside her. Her cheeks are almost the same shade of rose as her gown, and it makes the blue of her eyes even deeper. She doesn't look away. We're two stars held in each other's magnetic field, orbiting each other, unable to pull free.

I open my mouth to introduce myself.

Then a man steps into view next to her, his arm sliding around her waist and drawing her close. Her smile falters, the glow in her eyes dims, and her lashes veil her gaze.

He's familiar, this man. I have his dark eyes and his broad shoulders, though my hair is still black. His is salted with white.

He gives me a vicious smile, because he knows he's won this round in our endless battle. He saw my reaction to this woman and he knew what it meant. He knew what I wanted, and now he's smug in victory, since what I wanted he now has.

That beautiful woman is clearly his, and he makes that quite clear by pulling her even closer. All I'm left with is her last, burning glance before she allows my father to lead her away from the bar and back into the crowd.

CHAPTER ONE

Beatrix

THE LITTLE CASTILIAN church is packed to overflowing with members of Europe's most important aristocratic families, as well as the rich and the famous, all crowding in to say their goodbyes to Antonio Veracruz, tenth Duke of Riego, and also my husband.

I'm standing in the tiny little church alcove I discovered a few moments ago, needing a minute or two to catch my breath and adjust my black widow's veil over my face. The veil is partly for show and partly to hide my dry eyes, though I'm wondering why I'm bothering with it, since no one believes I'm truly mourning Antonio.

I know what they all think of me, all the ancient noble families of Spain and the rest of Europe. The rumours about me fill the gossip columns, internet forums, and social media posts. They say I'm a gold digger, a sugar baby, an escort, a courtesan. That I wrapped a poor old man's heart around my little finger and took all his money. I've even seen 'black widow' headlines and reports that I poisoned him to get my hands on the Veracruz estate…

Unfortunately for me, they're right. Not that I poisoned him—no, he died from a sudden and catastrophic heart attack—but they're right about the other thing. I am, in fact, a gold digger. Antonio knew that, though, and he was far from being a 'poor old man'.

We met through a company that provides rich people with 'companionship'. It's not an escort service or anything salacious, and the 'companionship' it promises is real. There's considerable vetting done if you want to register to be a 'companion' and many NDAs you have to sign.

I'd only just had my membership approved when I got a message from Antonio saying that he'd looked at my profile and wanted to meet me, with a view to my being his date at a charity fundraiser in London.

Not going to lie, I saw the words 'Spanish duke' and automatically said yes. I mean, when you have nothing except your looks, you can't afford to be picky. You have to do what you can to survive.

So I put on the one nice dress I had, and went along to the fancy London hotel he was staying in. We met in the bar and he bought me a drink. We chatted—I had made sure to read up on winemaking, since that was his passion—and we got on well enough that I went as his date to the fundraiser, before joining him on holiday in Greece.

We married soon after that, but our marriage wasn't about love. Antonio wanted someone he trusted to take over his estate after his death, plus he was lonely and didn't see why he couldn't have companionship in his later years. I was more than happy to provide that companionship if it meant my future would be taken care of. It was a mutually beneficial arrangement, and one I would have been totally happy about if it wasn't for one thing: Antonio's son.

I lean back against the cold stone of the alcove and shut my eyes, trying to even out my breathing. All the condolences and regrets people keep murmuring to me are difficult to handle, because I know they're all fake. No one means it. They all hate me.

I'm used to hate, though. It's just another thing I've learned how to protect myself from, since growing up in a series of neglectful foster homes will do that to a person. You either armour yourself or you don't survive, and luckily I know how to armour myself.

I'm going to need that armour today though, and not only to deal with a church full of people who view me with contempt, but also to deal with the other reason I'm here in this alcove, trying to get a breath.

Santiago Veracruz is here, Antonio's only son. Who hates me.

I thought he wouldn't come—I *prayed* he wouldn't come—but of course my prayers haven't been answered. I don't know why he's here when he and his father hadn't spoken for more than a year, and they had been estranged for much longer than that. Perhaps to make sure his father is really dead? Or maybe to stare at me hostilely the way he did the last time we met? Though it's probably about the will, and how Antonio cut him out of it, leaving him with nothing but an empty title, something Antonio didn't discuss with me until just before he died.

I'm not sure why Santiago hates me so much—it's not just about the will. It's got something to do with Antonio's acrimonious divorce from Santiago's mother years ago probably, and the fact that Antonio married me.

I didn't want to get involved in any family drama—the relationship between Antonio and his son had nothing to do with me—but I had no choice in the matter. Santiago involved me whether I wanted to be involved or not.

Then again, this wouldn't have been quite so bad if he hadn't been at that same London fundraiser that I attended with Antonio. If we hadn't locked eyes at the bar. If the taut, electric energy hadn't sprung between us and if he hadn't immediately come towards me with all his lethal, predatory grace…

I grit my teeth, trying to force those thoughts from my head.

I can't think of him, I can't. The service will be starting soon and I have to get my armour back in place, make sure there are no vulnerabilities. I can't afford them, not when it comes to him, because he'll use them against me to cause as much hurt as possible.

You've faced worse than him. Don't be a coward and start hiding now.

It's true, I have faced worse than him. While Antonio was alive I had some protection, but now that protection is gone and so all I have is myself.

It's all I've always had, after all.

'Ah, there you are,' a deep, dark masculine voice says, cold contempt running through the words. 'Practising your grieving-widow face?'

Every muscle in my body freezes and I open my eyes.

Of course, he's found me. Of course.

Through the black lace of my veil, I can see Santiago Veracruz standing in the entrance of the little alcove, completely blocking the exit. He's over six-three, with a body all hard muscle and lean, tensile strength. He's dressed in funereal black, the suit handmade and tailored perfectly to draw attention to his gladiator's shoulders, narrow waist and powerful thighs.

His face is a fallen angel's, both beautiful and cruel, with sharp cheekbones, a straight nose, and a hard mouth. His ink-black eyes are framed by thick, sooty lashes long enough to make a woman jealous, yet there's nothing soft in the way he's looking at me. Nothing kind. He's staring at me as if I'm dirt under his shoe.

I swallow, the gravitational force of his presence and the storm front of his hate almost palpable and pressing against me. I haven't seen him since that terrible incident a year ago, when he turned up at the estate not long after Antonio and I were married, to 'pay his respects', or at least that's what Antonio told me.

I didn't hear what was actually said, but I stood by the window and I could see Antonio and Santiago in the hacienda's driveway, shouting at each other in Spanish. Eventually, Santiago turned to leave and he caught sight of me, and his gaze was a black arrow, flaming with hate, aimed straight at my heart.

No, I know why he hates me. After that fundraiser, while I was in Greece with Antonio, I got a message from him. He must have investigated who I was and somehow found my email address. The message was short and sweet, asking for a meeting. But even as I read the email, even though part of me wanted nothing more than to meet him and see if the electricity I'd felt at the bar that night was still there and still mutual, the practical part of me, the survivor, warned me not to. That Santiago Veracruz had the power to ruin me, to make me his slave, and that's not something I could allow. The only power I've ever had is the power I have over myself, and the overwhelming attraction I felt for him that night felt like a threat to that power. If I wanted to live the life I'd planned for myself, I had to avoid him like the plague.

Except I can't avoid him right now, and even though Antonio isn't here to defend me any more, I'm not going to let the loathing of one hateful man get under my skin, no matter how he looks at me. I know how to protect myself. I haven't forgotten.

I push myself away from the wall and straighten, putting on the cold, hard mask that has been useful in the past when it comes to men. They don't generally like an ice queen, and steer clear.

'Santiago,' I say coolly. 'I didn't expect you to be here.'

'Whyever not?' He raises one black brow. 'I'm Antonio's only child after all.'

'So you're here to…what exactly? Surely not to offer your condolences?'

'No.' His inky eyes glitter. 'I only offer condolences to people who are genuinely grief-stricken, not those who perform for the crowd.'

Helpless anger simmers inside me. Normally I can manage my temper, but today is not a normal day. I didn't love Antonio and he didn't love me, but I'm upset that he's dead and I don't have the emotional energy to deal with Santiago's snide comments along with everything else.

'Interesting that you have thoughts about grief,' I snap, unable to stop myself, 'considering the last time you spoke to your father was a year ago and it was to shout at him.'

Santiago's black gaze doesn't even flicker. 'Tell me, how does it feel to know that everyone in this church thinks you're a murderess?'

I hate how his arrow hits its mark, no matter how well I armoured myself, and I hate how I want to shoot a few in return. I can't resist, even as it betrays me. 'How sweet,' I say acidly. 'I didn't know you cared about my feelings.'

He lets out a short, hard laugh. 'I don't.'

'So why are you here, then? If I didn't know any better I'd think you're looking to replace your father in my bed.' They're careless, heedless words, and as soon as they're out of my mouth I know I've made a mistake.

I shouldn't have acknowledged the electricity that still hums between us, even though it's been eighteen months since that night in London. I haven't forgotten. The electricity that I've never felt before or since, and never at all with Antonio. An electricity I have no control over and no choice about, and that I can't ever surrender to.

Fury leaps in Santiago's black eyes and he takes a step towards me. 'You wish,' he says, low and hard, his Spanish accent making music of the threat. 'No, Stepmother. I've come for something else.'

Stepmother? Really? Even though he's technically correct, I'm twenty-five and a good ten years younger than he is. And the way he loads the word, with as much contempt as he can, disdain dripping from every syllable…

Yet even as he says the words, my mouth goes dry. Because the smell of cold stone and incense is mixing with the warm, spicy scent that's all Santiago, and all I can think about is that night at the bar when he stood close to me. When that scent of his filled my head, and I regretted so much that I was here with someone else. That someone else having been his father, though I didn't know it then.

I swallow yet again, staring up at him through the black lace of my veil. I know why he's here, of course I know. 'This is about your inheritance, isn't it?'

'So sharp,' he purrs. 'You'll cut yourself if you're not careful.'

I ignore him. 'Your father left everything to me. And you know that.'

He takes another step forward, and I find myself taking a step back, trying to keep some distance between us. He's far too tall, looming over me, filling the alcove with his fierce, electric presence. 'I do know that,' he says silkily. '*Mi padre* was very clear.'

My heartbeat races and I hate the way I react to him. I hate how my body is springing to attention exactly the way it did that night, my skin tightening, something needy and desperate throbbing between my legs. Even when I saw him a year ago, through the window, the effect he had on me was the same.

But more than anything else, I hate how I feel as if I have no control over myself whenever he's near. Because it's dangerous to want things, especially things you can never and should never have.

'So?' I'm thankful for the veil that hides the sudden heat in my cheeks. 'There's nothing to discuss, Santiago.'

'*Mr Veracruz*, if you please,' he murmurs, looking down at me from his great height, his black eyes piercing me right through. 'You have not earned the right to my first name.'

I can hear the beat of my heart in my head, a loud thump in my skull. 'The service will be starting soon,' I say, hoping my voice sounds as hard and flat as his. 'So whatever you have to say—'

'Whatever I have to say,' he interrupts, stepping completely into the alcove and forcing me back against the stone wall, 'I will say right now, right here, my fucking father and his service be damned.'

The cold stone is at my back and I'm conscious of the warmth of the man at my front. He's like a furnace, radiating heat even as the flames in his black eyes are cold.

He lifts one hand and before I can stop him he flips back my widow's veil and looks down at me. 'Dry eyes,' he murmurs. 'I thought so.'

I want to snatch the veil back down to protect myself, but I won't give him the satisfaction of knowing how badly he rattles me. So instead I stare back, letting him see. 'I'm sad he's dead,' I say, because there's no point in pretending otherwise, not with him, 'but Antonio and I didn't love one another. We had an arrangement and that—'

'If it was money you wanted, you could have had mine,' Santiago snarls, suddenly fierce. He puts one hand on the stone either side of my head, slowly and deliberately, the black flames of his anger burning in his eyes. 'But you didn't want it, did you?'

I'm trembling, yet not with fright. Santiago is an intimidating man, but it's not him I'm afraid of. I'm afraid of this tense, burning thing between us, this irresistible pull, this need that I've never quite forgotten, no matter how hard I try. The one I can't ever talk about or name, because in the end it wasn't him I chose. It was his father.

He's too close and if he gets any closer I might lose myself, which again is why I didn't choose him. Antonio was always the safer choice for me.

'No,' I say huskily. 'I didn't. I wanted your father, not you. Now get out of my face.' I lift my hands, put them straight on his hard chest and push him away.

But he doesn't move.

And then something between us catches fire.

CHAPTER TWO

Santiago

HER SMALL HANDS land on my chest, the heat of her palms tearing through the wool and cotton of my clothes like a bullet tearing through flesh. My entire body tenses, every breath I have gone as a possessive, almost overwhelming physical desire floods through me.

I've wanted her from the moment I saw her at that fundraiser in London eighteen months ago. I didn't know then that my father was at the same fundraiser—I wouldn't have attended otherwise—or that she was there as his date. All I know is that the moment our eyes met, she was mine.

Except she wasn't mine. Because then my father turned up, sliding an arm around her waist and drawing her close. He knew I wanted her and she knew that too. But her own desire—her desire for me—she hid like the coward she is.

I did my due diligence. I found out just who and what she was, and I had the glorified sugar-baby matchmaking service she was registered with investigated. I have no issues with women who use their looks to make money and are upfront about it, because that's honest at least and I value honesty.

But Beatrix Morgan is not honest, and I know this because after that moment in London I contacted her through that sugar-baby company and asked her to meet me. We could have come to some mutually beneficial, not to mention very pleasurable arrangement, but she refused, telling me she didn't want me, that she preferred my father. I would have believed her if we hadn't had that moment at the bar. If I hadn't met her blue gaze and seen how the fire in her matched the fire in me. But that moment did happen and telling me she didn't want me made her a liar. And I despise liars.

Especially liars like my father. He was also petty, making sure that when he married her they had a big, splashy wedding. It was to spite me, which I could have forgiven him for, since I try never to let his many little slights get to me, but I couldn't forgive how it spited my mother, Catalina, too.

She'd been doing better after some time spent in a private facility in Switzerland that I paid an exorbitant amount for, and I'd been confident of her recovery. I'd just bought a house in Paris, her favourite city, and I'd been hoping she would be well enough to come and live with me.

Then came my bastard father's Society wedding to that pretty little liar, some forty years his junior, which my mother couldn't help but see reported in all the papers, and it sent her back down into another terrible bout of alcoholism.

So no, I couldn't forgive him for that. I couldn't forgive that blonde gold digger either. *Beatrix*. The girl from a glorified escort service, who married my father and stole my inheritance.

Not that I require that inheritance, not these days. I have more than enough money, with VZ Industries now the biggest research and development company in Europe. I'm branching into space engineering, providing development and design of various technologies to NASA and other private companies interested in space exploration. It's an exciting field to be involved with and I want to be at the forefront.

Yet all of that seems so unimportant right now. I'm a man who prides himself on his precision, his attention to detail, his ability to see both the big picture and the small, and whose self-control is paramount. Yet all I can think about is the feeling of Beatrix's palms on my chest. How she somehow took my fury and transmuted it into something molten and demanding, and next to impossible to control.

I only attended the funeral out of duty, not because I actually mourned Antonio. I spent too many years trying to build bridges with him, only to have him burn each and every one, so it's only a vague disappointment I feel now.

I certainly had no intention of speaking to the woman he married.

Except then I saw her disappear into the alcove and, no matter how hard I tried to resist the urge, like a proton drawn inexorably to an electron, I found myself drawn there too. And, once I was there, proximity turned into an intense chemical reaction that then burst into flame. I'd backed her up against the wall before I could stop myself.

I'm furious, naturally, and disgusted by my own need, by the sexual desire I can't seem to get a grip on. By the way I've backed her into a corner, unable to stop, and by the way I can't seem to drag my gaze from hers.

Her eyes are still the same deep blue, and her skin is still pale and smooth as cream. That perfect rosebud of a mouth has been haunting my dreams, and the tight black dress she's wearing outlines every one of her luscious, generous curves.

I don't know why she has this effect on me. She's beautiful, yes, but, as I told myself after she declined my offer of an affair, beauty I can get anywhere. There's no logical reason for the intensity of this desire—it's likely just chemicals and pheromones— so I'm appalled at myself and my behaviour. She's my stepmother, a woman my father has already had, and I'd never stoop to avail myself of his leavings.

Except she's looking up at me now, and beneath all the ice she radiates I can see heat in her blue eyes. No redness and her cheeks are dry, yet that blue has darkened, turning almost violet.

She wants me and we both know it, and that kicks my desire into overdrive, even as it makes me even more furious, both at myself and her.

It's unconscionable the way my body reacts. The

tightening of my muscles, the hardening of my cock, the roar of blood in my veins. I have many lovers, yet I've never wanted any of them as badly as I want her.

Except she chose Antonio over me. She chose a vengeful, bitter and selfish old man who could never satisfy any woman, let alone someone as young and attractive as she is. I'd never argue with a woman's choice, no matter how much I didn't like it, but the thing that gets to me about her is that she lied about that choice.

She's a coward and I should let her push me away, not stand here, relishing the heat of her palms on my chest and the delicate feminine musk of her scent. Yet I'm not letting her, and in this moment I suddenly understand why.

A part of me wants to get the truth from her one way or another.

I reach out and grip her jaw in my hand, her skin petal-soft against my fingertips, turning her face from one side to the other, staring at the pure lines of her cheekbones and arched blonde brows. Her straight nose. Her pretty, pretty mouth. I'm a scientist and so I need to discover what it is about her that gets me this hard, this hungry.

'When you were in bed with him,' I grind out, wanting to make her as furious as she makes me, 'did you have to fake it?'

She's trembling, but she makes no move to push me away again or to pull out of my grip. Her ice-queen mask is melting though—I can see the blue sparks of temper glitter in her eyes. 'No,' she says in her husky little voice, defiant still. 'He satisfied me completely.'

Another lie. My body is inches away from the warmth of hers, both of us held in place by the intensity of our need. 'Is that why you chose him?' I demand, even as some part of me is enraged at how I'm letting this despicable sexual jealousy get to me. 'Because he made you come?'

'What do you care?' she snaps back. 'Stop manhandling me.'

'You want me to manhandle you,' I snarl, keeping a tight grip on her. 'You're desperate for me to manhandle you.'

Her delicate jaw is in the palm of my hand, my thumb pressing into her cheek, and those blue sparks in her eyes are flames and they're burning high. Burning for me.

'Why would I want you?' Her gaze falls to my mouth and rises again. 'When I could have your father?'

It's a goad, and I shouldn't let such petty sexual insults get under my skin. I'm secure in my ability as a lover. I have nothing to prove, still less to her. Yet all I can think about now is showing her exactly why she should want me instead of him. Prove to her that she's lying and uncover the real truth.

I lean in closer, bare inches away from her luscious mouth. 'Too bad he's dead,' I murmur. 'What will you do now he's gone? You could come crawling to me, of course, but I'm afraid that ship has sailed. I don't do sloppy seconds.'

She's breathing very fast and I can see how her pulse races at the base of her throat, and without thought I loosen my grip on her chin, trailing my fingertips down the sides of her neck, before wrapping them around her throat, my palm pressing down gently on her pulse.

I should let her go, push myself away, turn my back on her once and for all, yet no matter how intensely I want this, I can't seem to make myself do it. Her skin is warm and silky, and her scent—some kind of flower—is intoxicating.

She gasps, her eyes darkening into the deepest violet, a night sky as the moon rises. 'Let me go,' she whispers. 'You don't want this.'

I don't. At all. But she hasn't given me the truth yet, and I will have it. 'Say stop,' I murmur. 'And I will.'

Her gaze drops once again to my mouth and I can feel her tremble. I can feel the pulse at the base of her throat beating hard against my palm. She swallows convulsively, her fingers curling into the wool of my jacket.

She does not say stop.

'You can't, can you?' I move closer, my body slowly pressing against hers. She's so soft and so very hot. 'I bet even now you're wet for me the way you were wet for me at the bar that night.'

'No,' she says in another husky little whisper. 'No, I'm not.'

The time for me to move away has long gone, and something primitive deep inside of me knows it. This is a reckoning the both of us have been circling for the past eighteen months, and now it's here we can't avoid it. It's fateful, almost. Promised, even.

I drop one hand to her hip and slide it slowly down the curve of her thigh over the top of her dress, her gaze trapped by mine. She's staring at me as if she'll fall to her death if she looks away, and I know I'll fall to mine if I don't touch her. So I ease my hand under the hem of her dress, finding the soft skin of her bare thigh, and then slide it higher, to the sensitive place between her thighs.

She shudders as I brush my fingers over the lacy fabric of her knickers, another breathy sound escaping her.

'Liar.' I press my fingertip against the soaking wet fabric, feeling her shake. 'When you were with him, did you imagine it was me? Is that how you got yourself off?'

There is colour in her cheeks now, a deep flush that only makes her lovelier, and she's trembling as I stroke her clit through her underwear. 'Yes,' she says hoarsely, the truth falling out of her. 'I mean…n-no.'

But it's too late, and we both know it.

A surge of base masculine satisfaction catches me, no matter how I fight it, which is something I'll castigate myself for later on. Now, though, I'm obsessed with this confession. Obsessed with how she's looking less and less like an ice queen and more and more like a wanton, desperate for a man's cock. For *mine*.

I remove my hand from between her thighs and lift it to her mouth, easing my finger into the wet heat between her lips. She doesn't resist, making another needy little sound as she tastes herself.

'That's how wet and hot you get when you think of me,' I tell her in a rough voice, now totally at the mercy of my own hunger, not to mention the hunger I can see in her eyes. 'That's how you taste when you want my cock inside you.'

Something leaps in her gaze then, a blaze of fury and desire in one hot, toxic flame, and her teeth close on my finger. Hard.

I mutter a curse, pulling my finger away, and then I do the only thing I can.

I cover her sharp mouth with mine, kissing her the way I've burned to do for eighteen long months.

CHAPTER THREE

Beatrix

I MAKE NO attempt to avoid his mouth. I can't, not now he's got one big hand gripping my throat, his long fingers pressed to my neck and his palm pressed to my pulse. And no matter how much I tell myself I don't want his kiss, I'm lying. I do want it. I want it with every breath in me.

The moment I touched him I knew I was lost, overwhelmed completely by his physical magnetism and my inability to resist it. He was not wrong when he said I wanted him to manhandle me. I do. I can't help it and I hate myself for it.

The same way I hate myself for imagining him instead of Antonio touching me, because he's right about that too. My relationship with Antonio was physical to a certain extent. He never insisted that I share his bed, but I knew he wanted me to. He was lonely, desperate for some physical comfort and warmth, and I felt sorry for him.

I know what it is to yearn for that comfort and

warmth. To yearn for touch, any kind of touch, just to remind you that you're real, that you exist, and that you're part of society and not merely living on the edges of it.

I wasn't experienced sexually. I was always careful around men, since a woman on her own with nothing and no one can be a target, but everything about our relationship was clear and upfront, and so I didn't feel unsafe. It cost me nothing to give him some physical comfort. I'm a little ashamed to admit that I pretended to be satisfied, but he was very male in his need to feel confident of his virility, and so I gave him that. Again, it cost me nothing.

Yet I know the moment Santiago's beautiful mouth covers mine that this is going to cost me everything. His kiss is rough, hot, demanding. A devastating force of nature that I can't do anything but surrender to, even though I know I shouldn't. Even though I know it's dangerous.

His tongue pushes into my mouth, where I can still taste myself, and now I can taste him too. It's the dark, forbidden flavour of everything you crave that you know is bad for you, but that you can't resist tasting again and again. And I can't resist it. I tilt my head back and give in. I want to kiss him back, but he won't let me, exploring my mouth hungrily and taking everything like a conqueror sacking the castle he's just captured.

There's a whole church full of people beyond this alcove, but I've forgotten all about them, too lost in the heat of his mouth and the devastation of his kiss to care.

His body is pressed to mine, and it's hot and so hard, and I'm rapidly forgetting all the lessons I've ever learned. How I can't let anyone get too close, let alone someone I hate. How precarious my life has been, and how I can't ever let anyone know that, especially not him. How this man could take everything away from me if he chooses to fight his father's will, because even with Antonio's money I don't have the resources that he does.

He owns one of the biggest private research and development companies in Europe, with millions of dollars at his disposal. I have nothing except the last will and testament of the husband who only married me so his son didn't end up with his assets.

Santiago reaches down again, sliding his hand over my thigh and back behind my knee, tugging my leg up and around his lean waist as he fits himself between my thighs. The length of his cock behind his fly presses against my sensitive clit, and he rocks his hips, causing sparks of a dark and dirty pleasure to light up every nerve-ending I have.

I can't let him do this to me. I can't. I ignored my desire for him, ignored the chemistry that I felt that night at the bar. I boxed it up and threw it into the darkest corner of my soul where I need never look at it again. Yet, despite all those 'can't's, I can't bring myself to push him away either.

I've never felt pleasure like this before, not once, and I want it with every fibre of my being, no matter how dangerous it is. And it is dangerous. Good things always are, because they can be taken away from you so easily. They can make you dependent, make you vulnerable, and that's something I should never allow.

But I'm helpless against this. I want something good for myself. Something's that's just mine, that I didn't have to give to anyone first or to work for. Everything I have I had to fight for, and I should be fighting for this too. But for the first time in my life all I want is to surrender.

'Oh, my God,' I whisper against his mouth as he rocks against me again, and I shiver in his grip, the pleasure splintering and fracturing inside me. 'Please...' I don't want to beg, it's too humiliating, but I can't stop the words from pouring out of my mouth. 'Oh...please...please...'

He does something to his trousers, then his hand is beneath my dress again and I feel him pull the fabric of my knickers roughly aside. Then he's pinning me to the hard stone at my back, pushing inside me, the big, hard length of his cock stretching me wide.

His mouth swallows my scream of pleasure, his kiss blinding as he grips my thigh, pulling it higher, working himself deeper. My fingers are curled, taking fistfuls of his jacket, my mouth under his total command as he begins to move, hard and deep. He's rough, urgent, desperate and so am I. Dimly I'm aware that we're in public, that someone could walk by and find us at any moment, and that should horrify me. Yet right now the thought only adds extra spice to the already agonising physical pleasure.

I have never wanted anything more than I want him right now, and if I was in my right mind I'd be appalled at myself and what I'm doing. By how I'm losing my virginity to the man who's technically my stepson, in the alcove of a church during my husband's funeral.

But I'm not in my right mind and the movement of his hips as he thrusts into me, demanding and hungry, is making me want to scream. I cling to his jacket and sink my teeth into his full bottom lip as the pleasure turns me inside out. He growls, biting me back, his fingers around my throat tightening a fraction. Not enough to hurt or to choke, just enough to make sure I feel them like a collar around my neck. A collar denoting his ownership.

He moves faster, harder, changing the angle of his thrusts, and without warning the pleasure cracks and spiderwebs around me, glass under pressure breaking as the climax hits. I give another hoarse scream that he stems with his mouth, before shuddering as it takes him too, his rough groan of release vibrating against my lips.

There's a moment of deafening silence and all I can hear is the thunder of my own heartbeat. He's warm and solid, still gripping me tight, and for a second I forget who he is to me. When I only want to rest against him, let his heat and solidity protect me from the rest of the world.

Then slowly, but surely, reality winds a cold thread through me. This is Antonio's funeral and we're in a church, and I've just had sex with my stepson. And if anyone found us here like this…

If I'm hated now, that would be nothing compared to the hate I'd get for that. He would be fine—men always are—but I would be vilified. That shouldn't matter to me—I have my armour after all—but all that hate gets to you after a while. Not being respectable enough. Not being well behaved enough. Not being good enough.

All I wanted after the funeral was to retire to the Veracruz estate and disappear from public view, safely insulated by Antonio's money. Then what I'd planned, once the immediate battle for survival had been won, was to decide how I wanted the rest of my life to look. I want to go back to complete the education I never finished. I want to go to university. I want a career. I want a family…

But all of that won't happen if I'm caught.

Panic sits cold and sharp inside me and I shove a little desperately at him. 'Please,' I murmur, in the exact opposite tone to how I begged him not five minutes ago. 'Let me go.'

For a moment he's still, then abruptly he withdraws, stepping back and tucking himself away, zipping up the fly of his trousers. I scrabble about, pushing my dress down to cover myself.

He's staring at me and if I didn't know any better the expression on his face looks like one of shock. But I do know better. This is Santiago Veracruz and I have just lost the virginity his own father never managed to take, to him. And he hates me.

I can't bear to hear whatever words are going to

come out of his mouth once his shock has worn off, so I pull down my veil and push past him, heading straight to the front of the church just in time for the service.

CHAPTER FOUR

Santiago

I STARE DOWN at my phone screen, at the words in stark black and white. It's a text from Sofia, my family's housekeeper, who still manages the Veracruz estate and who has had a soft spot for me ever since I was a child.

Every so often she'd pass on information to me, mostly about my father, since she never agreed with his demonisation of me, and she worried about some of his decisions regarding the estate. She has no love for the new Duchess either, which is presumably why she just texted me with: Señora Beatrix has been sick for the past six weeks and finally she went to the doctor. She said nothing when she returned, but the rumours in the village say she's pregnant.

Something that has been nagging at me for the past four months now hardens into stone, with sharp edges that cut. And I know what it is.

Certainty.

I lean back in my chair and stare unseeing at the

opposite wall of my office in the VZ Industries building, trying to force myself to sit still. There's no need to leap into a helicopter and fly from Paris straight to Castile immediately, no need whatsoever. Just because it concerns Beatrix, it doesn't mean the situation needs my instant and personal attention.

I grit my teeth, forcing the urge to go into submission, and eventually, when it doesn't, I shove my chair back and start pacing. I always do my best thinking while in motion.

As much as I want to, there's no point castigating myself for what happened four months ago. I'm well aware of how badly my self-control failed. What matters now, though, are the facts and those are that Beatrix is likely pregnant and, while there's a slight chance that Antonio is the father, the more obvious candidate is myself.

I didn't use a condom that day at the funeral, too overcome by my own base urges to even think about it. I didn't even remember not using one, just had that nagging feeling for months that I was missing something.

Turns out, I *was* missing something and now that lapse of memory has come back to bite me.

A child. *My* child.

Something flexes and shifts inside me in response, something powerful and possessive. The little piece of my father that I've never quite managed to get rid of, that yearns and wants and hungers for things I can't permit myself to have.

I despise that part of myself, and *she* called to it

back there at the funeral. She brought it out of me, and I wasn't strong enough to overcome it. But that won't happen again. Emotions always come second to my intellect, since emotions are weaknesses, little vulnerabilities that allow all sorts of other, more primitive things to creep in, such as addiction, sexual excess, violence. Those things ruined my parents and I won't permit them to ruin me.

My intellect, on the other hand, is cool and rational. It favours facts, not instincts, and it is only wrong when the facts are wrong. My intellect has saved me more times than I can count, especially when I was growing up, and it's certainly more trustworthy than my parents ever were.

After all, one of the many reasons I hated my father was that he had no control over himself. He had a ready temper that he'd lose at the slightest provocation, and base sexual urges that led him into the affairs that so humiliated my mother.

She loved him, that was her problem. She'd always been emotionally fragile, and finding out about his affairs broke her. Some of the blame for that does lie with me, I admit, since I was the one who told her about them, after discovering Antonio with one of his mistresses. She tried to talk to him, but he was already furious with me for what he deemed 'a betrayal of trust' in informing her, and threw her out, throwing me out along with her.

I have some regrets about telling her, since her alcohol addiction started not long after their marriage ended. But I was only a child at the time—twelve, if not younger—and I was angry at my father for his betrayal and thought she should know he'd been lying to her. Those regrets are small ones, however, since she'd have found out at some point anyway, and the result would have been the same.

I pace over to the window and stop a moment, staring out at the winding silver strip of the Seine and the spire of Notre Dame.

I could choose to ignore her pregnancy, and tell myself that the child is my father's rather than mine. Leave her to bring up the baby in the peace of the Veracruz's Castilian estate. But I know myself. I won't be able to let this go until I know for sure whose child it is.

The facts need to be ascertained. They're vital in my work as a scientist. Facts are the building blocks of the universe, they make up the fabric of reality, inexorable as gravity, and more importantly, they don't lie. People do, though. People do nothing but lie and most especially when it comes to protecting their own interests. And they hate the truth, too. My father, for example, did not like me telling the truth, and the fact that he got rid of me when he got rid of my mother made a lie out of all the words of love he once gave us.

He didn't love us at all. He didn't love her and he didn't love me, and so I can never trust those words ever again. People in general can't be trusted, and so I put my faith in the facts.

I can't ignore those facts now. The child will either be mine or be my half-sibling, and I must know which it is in order to make a plan about what to do next.

For that I'll need a paternity test. My father's widow

won't like that, especially if she's trying to hide the pregnancy, which she clearly is, considering she hasn't told anyone about it. But that's too bad. I will have to insist.

And if the child is yours?

I stare at my reflection in the glass, trying not to see my father's features looking back at me. At least my mother's endless need for attention isn't visible. There's too much of both of them in me for comfort, though. It's why I made the decision early on that I would never have children of my own. I have too many bad genes, too many vulnerabilities to pass on.

Except if this child is mine I'll need to make a choice about what to do.

I've always been a man who takes responsibility for his mistakes. It's why I took responsibility for my mother's health, why I look after her even now, since I'm the one who told her about my father's affairs. And, since I'm the one who made the mistake and forgot the condom, I'll take responsibility for any child resulting from that mistake.

What that responsibility looks like, I can't determine as yet. What I do know is that I won't make any decisions until I know for certain who the father of Beatrix's child is.

Taking out my phone, I scroll through my list of contacts. I have her number and email address saved after that abortive attempt to convince her that she needed to choose me instead of Antonio. I should have deleted it long ago, but I didn't. I thought it might come in useful one day, and it looks like today is that day.

You saved it because you couldn't quite let go of her, could you?

Hardly. I let her go the day she married my father.

Is that why you backed her up against the wall in the church the day of your father's funeral? Because you'd let her go?

I ignore the whispers in my head, they're not relevant, and hit the call button instead.

'Hello?' she says, answering immediately, and no matter how long it's been since I heard her husky little voice, the effect it has on me is the same.

Every muscle in my body tenses and all I can think about is that same voice begging me in the church as I pushed inside her, *'Please...oh, please...'*

I grit my teeth, forcing my body's urges back into the box they came from. 'Miss Morgan,' I say, deliberately not using her married name. 'It appears we need to have a little chat.'

There's a silence down the other end of the phone.

I didn't tell her it was me calling, but she'll know. She remembers my voice just as I remember hers. She'll be shocked to hear from me, no doubt, and is probably hoping that I'm calling her about something else and not the pregnancy she deliberately didn't tell me about.

'Santiago,' she says eventually, her tone admirably cool. 'Or should I say, *Mr Veracruz*? How nice of you to call. What would you like to chat about?'

Oh, she's good. She's very good. Perfect even, especially with that faint note of surprise at the end.

Another person might think she's being genuine, but I know better.

'Come, now, Miss Morgan,' I turn away from the window and pace over to my desk, 'let's not pretend. I know about your pregnancy.'

Again, there's a silence and this time it's a shocked silence.

I smile as I pull out my chair and sit down. I'm enjoying this. I'm enjoying rattling the ice-queen mask that she likes to pretend is the truth of her. But that's not the truth. There's a wild heat in her and now I know that for a fact. I tasted it.

'What pregnancy?' She sounds unbothered, but I know she is, indeed, very bothered. There's a roughness to her voice that she can't hide. 'I don't know what you're talking about.'

'Still lying through your teeth, I see,' I say. 'Don't play games with me, Miss Morgan. The rumours are all through the village and you've been sick for approximately six weeks. That's a long time for a stomach bug.'

She's quiet a moment, then says, with a slight hint of impatience, as if I'm a child pestering her for a sweet, 'Okay, fine. Yes, I'm pregnant. I was hoping to wait a little longer to announce it formally. Who told you? Sofia, I suppose?'

I ignore this, conscious of a rising fury that she doesn't seem perturbed to have been caught in a lie. 'You didn't think that perhaps I might have wanted to know?' I demand roughly.

'And why would you want to know?' she asks, as if she can't think of one single reason.

I grip my phone hard, the edges digging into my palms as the fury mixes with the raw desire I always feel for her, eating through my self-control like hydrochloric acid through metal. 'We had sex without a condom,' I say bluntly. 'Why do you think I'd want to know?'

She gives a long-suffering sigh, as if this conversation is boring her. 'It was once,' she says. 'And surely you must know that your father and I shared a bed. The baby is his, not yours.'

It could be. It very well could be. And yet some instinct in me is telling me she's lying, and this only makes my fury burn even hotter. Is she lying because she thinks I'm not a fit father for the child? That there's something wrong with me?

You know there is. There always has been.

I almost growl as I shove the thought away. 'I only have your word for that,' I say, struggling to keep my temper under control. 'And I know how much your word is worth.'

'Are you calling me a liar, Mr Veracruz?' she enquires coolly.

'It's not the first time you've been called one, remember?'

This time she says nothing, but I can feel the hot electric current between us pull tight, and it doesn't matter that she's thousands of miles away in Spain while I'm here in France. I can feel it, I'm sure she can feel it too, and I'm not above using that to get what I want.

'Remember how you told me that you didn't want me?' I go on, lowering my voice, turning it into a caress. 'Remember how wet you were and how desperately you begged me to make you come?'

I hear her take a soft, shaken breath and a savage satisfaction twists inside me. 'You lied about that,' I say. 'I wouldn't put it past you to lie about this too.'

Again, she says nothing.

'A paternity test.' I make no effort to hide the demand in my voice. 'I want one.'

'Go to hell,' she says.

And abruptly ends the call.

CHAPTER FIVE

Beatrix

I'M WALKING OUT of the hacienda's kitchen at the Veracruz estate, when I hear the rhythmic sound of helicopter rotors. I stop dead, listening as it gets louder and louder, my pulse ramping up. The only person I know who'd use a helicopter to get anywhere died four months ago, which means it's obviously not Antonio. So who else could it be? And why would they be flying to this remote spot in Castile? We don't get visitors, since I've yet to make friends with anyone in Spain. I had none in England, either, or not close friends, but that was because it was easier not to have any. I wanted a home first, a place where I was going to stay permanently—making friends when you're constantly moving around is difficult. Another lesson from my numerous foster homes.

I move quickly along the hacienda's wide, whitewashed hallways to the central courtyard, then make my way down the colonnade to the rear of the house. There's a big salon there that runs the width of the hacienda, with windows that look out over the rolling lawns and gardens, and as I reach those windows a black helicopter comes in to land directly on the lawn. There's a logo on the doors and, while I'm too far away to see what it is, a sudden premonition grips me.

You know exactly who this is.

Cold pours through my veins, icy as snow melt, because of course I know.

It's Santiago Veracruz. Who else could it possibly be?

He called me out of the blue yesterday, telling me he knew about the pregnancy, and, though he didn't answer my question when, struggling to conceal my shock, I asked him who'd told him, I knew all the same. Sofia, the housekeeper who's worked for the Veracruz family for years and doesn't like me, must have passed it on. Not that I've done anything to her, but she's been deeply suspicious of me since I married Antonio and has remained so.

I don't blame her, considering all the rumours about me—gold digger taking advantage of a poor old man et cetera. But she didn't know the truth about Antonio and me, that we had an agreement and one that Antonio didn't want known. Like most Spanish men, he wanted everyone to think that he was virile enough to snare a pretty, young woman, and, since I needed his money, I went along with it.

But I'm tired of the constant stream of hate that flows in my direction, and the last few weeks I've been feeling so sick that I don't have the emotional energy to confront her about it. I don't have the energy to confront Santiago, either, and that's no one's fault but my own.

If I were a better liar he'd have believed me when I told him the baby was Antonio's. If I were a better liar I wouldn't be in this situation in the first place. I'd have shoved him away that day in the church before he could get any closer to me, but…

I didn't. Antonio never managed to perform in bed—Santiago was right about that—so of course the baby isn't his. And here I am, pregnant with Santiago's child and that's my fault. What I was afraid of happening, did happen. He overwhelmed my self-control so completely I didn't even think about stopping him, or about protection either. So when I first started feeling sick in the mornings and more tired than usual, a pregnancy didn't even occur to me.

Soon, though, it became clear that it wasn't the flu, that it was more than that, and an appointment with the village doctor soon proved it. The timing is terrible and the father being who he is makes things even worse, but even so, as soon as I found out, I knew I'd be keeping the baby. There was never going to be any other decision for me.

My birth mother died having me and my birth father put me into foster care almost as soon as I was born, so I have no family. But this baby is my blood, the only blood I have, and I want it with every breath in me. We'll be a family together, and now I have a home, we'll also have a place to belong.

The Veracruz estate, with its orange groves, whitewashed hacienda, rolling lawns, and village just down the road, will be that place. No cheap, mouldy, mildewed flats or bedsits too small to even turn around in. No couches of casual acquaintances when the rent money runs out, or food banks when the food money runs out too.

My child will have this beautiful house to call home, and they'll be brought up speaking Spanish, and they'll make friends with all the kids in the village. They'll never be alone the way I was alone

I don't want Santiago to be part of that, though, which isn't very sympathetic of me, and I know that. But I'm sure that if he ever finds out that the child is his, he'll take it away from me. Which is why I can't take that paternity test he demanded, because the results will make it very clear he's the father. And I can't let him find out. This child is mine and I'm keeping it. When the child is older, I'll tell him or her who their father is, but not until later. Much, much later.

Out on the lawn, the helicopter settles on the grass, then the door opens, and a very tall man leaps out. He strides across the lawn in the direction of the hacienda, and yes, there's no mistaking him. It's Santiago and he's no doubt here to demand that paternity test he mentioned on the phone yesterday.

I suppose he has a right to ask for one, but I have no idea why he'd even care if the child is his or not. Family's clearly not that important to him or else he and Antonio would have made up long ago—not that Antonio gave me any real details about why he seemed to hate his son so much. He only ever said that that Santiago was cold, heartless, and a terrible son, and that he would never forgive him for 'what he did'. Whatever that was. I didn't press, since it seemed to be a sensitive topic, and I didn't want to get involved anyway.

Certainly, Antonio was right about one thing: Santiago *is* cold and heartless, and I'm dreading seeing him again.

I take a steadying breath, and try to find my usual icy mask. My heartbeat is racing, but I ignore it as I sit myself down on one of the salon's deep, comfortable sofas. Pulling a magazine from the coffee table in front of me into my lap, I leaf through it as if I've been sitting here for hours peacefully reading. So when the doors open and Santiago strides in, I'm more than calm. More than ready to deal with him.

Except then I look up, and I realise that I'm not ready to deal with him at all, because he's in a suit of midnight blue, his shirt black, his tie a splash of crimson, and the room is full of the force of his electric presence.

His black eyes pin me to the sofa cushions, and for a moment all I can think about are those desperate minutes four months earlier in the church. When his hand gripped my throat as he pushed inside me, his hot mouth devouring me even as I tried to devour him. All that heat and hunger overwhelming us both.

He's thinking the same thing, too, I can tell, because his dark gaze loses its chill, turning into a blaze of heat that sears me all the way through.

Antonio wasn't *right. He's not cold at all.*

'Miss Morgan,' he says with icy formality, his voice betraying none of the heat in his gaze.

'Mr Veracruz,' I reply in the same tone, trying to ignore the thunder of my heart and the flames in his eyes. 'To what do I owe the pleasure?'

'You know why I'm here. Let's not play this game.'

I glance down at the magazine in my lap and turn the page slowly, taking my time so my hands don't shake. 'I presume this has something to do with the conversation we had yesterday?'

'Yes.' The word is sharply bitten off.

I turn another page. 'And I suppose you want—'

Except I don't get to finish as the magazine is abruptly jerked from my fingers. 'Excuse me?' I demand in outrage, looking up at him and forgetting that I'm supposed to be cool and calm. 'What the hell are you doing?'

Santiago throws the magazine back onto the coffee table and folds his arms across his broad chest. He's standing right in front of me now, towering over me the way he likes to do, and I realise I made a mistake in sitting down. 'The paternity test,' he snaps. 'I want it done.'

I swallow and fold my hands in my lap, trying not to let him get to me. 'If you recall,' I say coolly, 'I told you to go to hell.'

'That is not an option.' His expression is like granite, no give in it whatsoever. 'If there is the slightest chance that the baby is mine, I want to know about it.'

A thread of panic winds through me and I have to grip my hands together hard, fighting it. 'There is no chance of the baby being yours.' I keep my voice calm and absolutely certain. 'Antonio is the father.'

Santiago's inky gaze bores a hole through me and I try not to flinch away. One little slip and he'll know I'm lying through my teeth.

'Liar,' he says, and instantly my brain returns to the church again, his finger stroking me, finding me wet as he knew I would be. *Liar,* he'd said then, too.

His eyes glitter. He's remembering that same moment, the moment I betrayed myself, and now the air between us is getting hot, taut, electric. Closing around me, stealing my breath, and making my skin tighten.

'Why do you keep lying?' he murmurs in that dark, caressing tone he used yesterday on the phone when he accused me of the same thing. 'When you know I can tell?'

I take a breath, hoping it isn't as audible as I'm afraid it is, then say, icily, 'I'm not lying. Why do you care if the baby is yours anyway?'

Something I can't read flickers across his handsome face, then it's gone. 'Because I, unlike some people, take responsibility for my mistakes.'

A hot burst of anger floods through me all of a sudden, and before I know what I'm doing I shove myself up off the couch so I'm standing in front of him. 'My baby is *not* a mistake,' I say fiercely. 'And I won't have you saying it is.'

The flames in his eyes leap higher and I realise all at once that I'm standing too close to him. That we're bare inches apart and I can smell the delicious scent of his aftershave, feel the warmth of his body, and the desperate, needy thing inside me, the part of me that's never sated, quivers with anticipation.

I'm not giving in to it, not again, so I try to go past him, to put some distance between us, but he puts out a hand, stopping me in my tracks. 'Don't you dare walk away,' he says in a low, hard voice. 'This is a conversation we are going to have whether you want to have it or not.'

I can't look him in the eye—I'm too afraid of what he'll see and I've already betrayed myself enough as it is—so I stare at the hand blocking my path instead. 'There's nothing to talk about. You want a paternity test and I have refused. End of conversation.'

His hand moves and somehow I know what he's going to do, and that I could move if I wanted to avoid it. But I don't move. The needy part of me makes me stand still as he takes my jaw in that big hand of his, forcing me to look up at him. His fingers are warm on my skin and I can feel his strength. He could snap my neck with a simple twist of his hand, yet his hold is surprisingly gentle.

His gaze roves over my face, but what he's trying to find I don't know. Perhaps evidence of my lies, which, of course, he'll discover, because, as it turns out, I'm a terrible liar, especially when it comes to him.

'What are you so afraid of?' he asks, the hard note in his voice softening slightly. 'Finding out that the child *is* actually mine?'

I hate that I've given myself away yet again, that he's seen the panic I've been trying to hide. I'm desperate to tell him that I'm afraid of nothing and that he needs to stop putting his hands on me, but my voice won't work. The needy part of me wants more of that note of softness, as if it matters to him that I'm afraid, and it wants more of his touch, craves the heat of it, the feeling of being desired.

But I can't surrender to that part of myself. It's too desperate, and because it has no defences it's far too vulnerable. What it wants it can never have and never will. I won't allow it. I gave in to it once before, when I was thirteen and I was placed with a truly wonderful foster family. I wanted to stay with them so badly, and I really believed they were going to end up adopting me, but they didn't. They adopted another girl instead, and I never knew why they wanted her instead of me. It took me years to recover from the hurt, and I'll never let it happen again. I'll never let myself want anything too much, and I'll never let anyone in only for them to turn around and devastate me.

So I harden my heart and force my cravings away. 'Why would I be afraid?' I arch a brow. 'The child *isn't* yours.'

But his sharp gaze is relentless. 'We could argue about this all day, I'm sure, but I haven't got the time. I'm due in Paris for a meeting first thing in the morning, and, since I'm not leaving without an answer, if you don't give me one you'll be coming with me.'

Shock echoes through me. 'But you can't—'

'Oh, I assure you that I can, Miss Morgan. And I will.' His hand on me tightens minutely and my breath catches hard. I want to pull away from him, jerk myself out of his grip, slap his face for his audacity, but my body simply won't obey. Instead I stand there, staring up at him, captured by the darkness of his eyes and the bright, hot electricity that fills the air around us.

'That will involve kidnapping,' I say, my voice gone husky. 'And I'm sure the police will have something to say about that.'

'I don't need to kidnap you.' A soft roughness has entered the words, as if he's as affected by our chemistry as I am. 'You'll come willingly enough.'

'Oh, will I?' I swallow against his palm, my mouth dry. 'Give me one good reason.'

'You're a passionate woman, Miss Morgan.' His black gaze stares into mine, hypnotic as a snake charmer's. 'I know exactly how passionate. And four months is a long time to go without a man. In which case, I'm prepared to offer you my services in bed, in return for agreeing to the paternity test.'

CHAPTER SIX

Santiago

HER BLUE EYES have gone wide, the frantic beat of her pulse racing beneath my thumb. It was a mistake to touch Beatrix and I know it. I was getting frustrated with her lies, and I wanted to see the expression on her face, see what she was trying to hide, because she was avoiding my gaze for a reason.

Yet now her warm skin is beneath my fingertips and her delicate scent is wrapping itself around me, and I can see how her gaze darkens.

Fuck, I should be learning from all these mistakes I keep making with her, yet I'm not.

After she hung up on me yesterday, I debated what to do for some time. I could have called her back, but I knew she'd only ignore me, so I dismissed that idea. A visit seemed in order, and a personal one at that, since I had to impress upon her the importance of the test, and if necessary drag her all the way back to Paris to get it done.

Yet when I came in she was so cool, so calm, flicking through a magazine, not even deigning to look at me. It infuriated me. My temper was already on edge from having to make this quite unnecessary trip, and I had to pull the magazine away from her to get her attention.

Her blue gaze was cold, but I could see the fire lurking beneath all that ice. Especially when I told her the baby was a mistake. That drove her up onto her feet, the ice melting, fury glittering brightly in her eyes.

She clearly didn't like me saying that, though for what reason I'm not sure. But then she tried to walk away from me, and I wasn't having that. She's done that twice to me now, first after our interlude at the church, and second, hanging up on me during our phone conversation. There will not be a third, so I stopped her. Then I reached out and took her jaw in my hand and forced her gaze to meet mine. I wanted to see what was in her eyes, ask her just what her issue with the paternity test was, especially if she's so certain the baby isn't mine.

That's when I saw her fear. I caught only a fleeting glimpse before she managed to hide it, but it was there. Her fear shouldn't have mattered to me, nor should I be curious about it, except if it was fear of taking the paternity test itself I need to know why.

Yet then came the moment that always comes when we get close. When physical awareness of each other impinges on and blots out everything else. The softness of her skin, the delicate scent of flowers, the flickering hunger beneath the ice in her eyes. The raging electricity that crackles and sparks when we touch.

It was enraging to find it still burning, yet it was impossible to deny. And, since I knew that self-restraint hadn't worked, there was only one other possible solution: feed the hunger until I'm not hungry any more.

Hence my offer to her. I know she wants me, that she can't resist me, and I know that she hates our chemistry as much as I do. This is a chance for her to set fire to it, let it burn away completely until there's nothing but ashes left. And in return, she'll take the test willingly.

'Your "services"?' she echoes, shock in her eyes.

Does she really not know what I'm talking about? When I made the same offer to her eighteen months ago?

'Come, now, Miss Morgan,' I say. 'Do I really have to explain myself? You know exactly what I mean.'

Her pulse has picked up, I can feel the beat of it against my thumb. The shock in her eyes is giving way to a mix of fury and—yes, I can see how the blue darkens into tell-tale violet—desire. She doesn't want to want me the way I don't want to want her, but we're both helpless against it all the same.

'How dare you?' she says, quivering with rage. 'I'm not a sex worker.'

'Are you not?' I ask. 'Didn't my father pay you for your services?' I don't care that he did—after all, I offered her the same deal. No, I'm only asking out of curiosity.

Her cheeks flush with colour, her eyes glittering like stars. 'It wasn't like that,' she says in a tight voice. 'I chose to have sex with him.'

But I'm not interested in what it was 'like' with

him. I don't care about him, not any more. What I want is her.

The more I think about it, the more certain I become. I should have realised this four months ago in the church, when my self-control failed, that having her is the only way. Her in my bed for however long it takes us to finally get rid of this chemistry. It's basic logic.

'Just like you chose to have sex with me,' I point out. 'Or are you going to lie again and say you didn't want me? That you didn't beg when I had my hand between your thighs?'

She pulls herself out of my grip then, yet doesn't sidestep me. Instead she stays exactly where she is, far too close to me, and lifts her chin, proud as any queen. 'I see.' One golden brow lifts. 'So would this be for my benefit or yours?' She leans in a little, her blue gaze on mine. 'I bet if I was to put my hand between *your* thighs, you'd be hard.'

If she thinks that giving me a taste of what I gave her will win this particular confrontation, she'd be wrong. Unlike her, I'm honest about what I want and I see no reason to hide it. Not when the truth is so obvious.

'Why not find out?' I invite silkily. 'Don't be shy.'

Are you sure this is what you want to do?

Naturally, I'm sure. It's the most logical solution to a reprehensible situation. I would rather not feel this hunger for her, but it is what it is. I feel it and so does she, and feeding the hunger is the best answer. It doesn't mean I'm addicted. It doesn't mean I'm helpless against my baser urges. *I* have made the decision, not my cock, and as far as I'm concerned, my intellect is still in full control.

Her gaze drops to my fly, then back up again, cool and calm as a frozen sea. 'No, thank you,' she says, as if I'm offering her a cup of tea she doesn't want. 'I'd rather not.'

I almost admire her response. Respect even, that she's working so hard to pretend she doesn't want me with everything in her. But the darkness of her eyes, those flickers of violet, give her away. She wants to touch me. She's desperate to touch me.

You want her to touch you, too.

Oh, I do. But I'm not desperate. I can wait.

I smile, letting her know that I can see all the way through her. 'You need more to sweeten the deal? Fine. Multiple orgasms *and* money. Whatever my father was paying you, I'll double it.'

Her jaw tightens, hot sparks of temper melting the ice in them. 'I *don't* want you,' she insists. 'And I don't want your money.'

'What do you want, then?' I'm growing impatient with the conversation. If she continues to argue, I'll throw her over my shoulder and carry her to the helicopter myself. I do not have the time for yet more protests.

A bright blue flame burns suddenly in her eyes. 'I want to keep my baby. That's what I want.'

Something shifts inside me, something unfamiliar, and once again I find myself reluctantly admiring her stubborn determination. She has a…strength of character that I wasn't expecting, and the scientist in me is intrigued. It likes a puzzle. Still, what's between us is merely physical, simple chemistry, and no matter how much of a puzzle she is, I won't be following up on it.

However, I'm going to have to think about her demand. Because, while I'm sure I *am* the father, the test will prove it, and once it does I'll have to make some decisions about what I want when it comes to the child. But I'm not going to do that until I have all the facts. There are too many variables to account for now.

'I shall take that under advisement,' I tell her testily, because I'm impatient to get going. 'I need all the facts before I make you any promises.'

She lifts her chin. 'I don't care what you need. If you don't give me your word that the baby stays with me, then I'm not going anywhere.'

Damn, stubborn woman. How she knows that giving my word is a sacred vow I have no idea, but she does. 'You would trust my word?' I ask, since, for all my protests, I *will* follow up on this particular curiosity.

'I trust your honesty,' she says, 'seeing as how it's clearly important to you.'

She's not wrong. People are sometimes difficult to read, which is why honesty is vital and why I demand it from my employees, colleagues, and from my lovers. I demand it from myself too, so giving my word now means I'll have no choice but to keep it.

Allowing her to keep the child will cost you nothing.

It won't and I know that intellectually. Yet something inside me, the strange, powerful and possessive urge that gripped me the moment I knew she was pregnant, is shifting inside me again. It's angry, this thing, and it's telling me that the child is mine too, and any decision about said child has to be made with my input.

I'm not a possessive man. Possessiveness implies want, which, apart from the sexual desire I have for Beatrix, I don't feel. Of course, I want to solve the present difficulties we're having with the propulsion system of a new rocket we're developing, but that is ambition. I don't want to own the breakthrough—that will be for the good of the world, not for my personal monetary gain—but I certainly *want* to be the one who makes that breakthrough.

Except this is different. This possessiveness goes deeper than ambition or even desire. It's a biological response, hard-wired into my DNA, and the scientist knows it's impossible to ignore. Regardless of the fact that I never wanted children, I *will* be a father, and I *want* the child. *My* child.

But she won't go willingly with you unless you promise her.

Furiously, I think once again about picking her up, tossing her over my shoulder and carrying her off. It would certainly end this ridiculous discussion once and for all. But dragging her kicking and screaming to the helicopter holds no appeal, and so I do the only thing I can.

'Very well,' I say. 'The child will stay with you.'

'Your word, *Mr Veracruz*,' she says, enunciating my title in a way that gets under my skin like a burr. 'I'm not going anywhere until I get it.'

'I *promise* the child will stay with you,' I say, enunciating the word right back, and then, because I'm not giving up on this idea of getting rid of our mutual hunger once and for all, I add, 'on one condition.'

Her eyes widen fractionally. 'You don't have the right to—'

'This baby is *mine*,' I interrupt. 'And once the formalities have been completed and the results are clear without a shadow of a doubt, I will claim it. I won't take it away from you, but if you want to stay with it, there is only one way you may do so: in my bed.'

Her temper glitters, angry sparks leaping in her eyes. 'So that's how you're going to handle this? You're going to blackmail me into bed?'

'Is it really blackmail when you're desperate to be there?' I meet her gaze head-on. 'One way or another, pretty Beatrix, that's where you're going to end up and we both know it.'

The colour in her cheeks has deepened, the blue of her eyes hot with fury, yet I can see the violet of her desire, it's burning there too, making a liar out of all her protestations.

'You just can't stand him winning, can you?' she says, low and furious. 'Even now he's gone.'

'This has got nothing to do with him,' I snap, because of course she means Antonio. 'This is about you and me.'

She takes a breath. 'I thought you didn't want "sloppy seconds"?'

The way she throws my own ill-chosen words back at me does nothing for my temper. Especially when I did, in fact, want his sloppy seconds and still do.

'Enough,' I say in a hard voice. 'I have no time for

petty arguments. I have given you my promise; now I want yours.'

There is no sign of the ice maiden in her now, her eyes burning and her cheeks burning along with them. She's furious with me, doesn't want to give in, yet she wants the baby, and, whether she likes it or not, she wants me, too.

'I hate you,' she says flatly.

'That's the first honest thing you've said all day,' I say in the same tone.

She mutters something vicious under her breath, then finally says, 'Okay, I promise. Now, let's get this over with.'

CHAPTER SEVEN

Beatrix

MY STOMACH IS tying itself in knots as we come in to land in Paris, the setting sun giving the City of Lights a beautiful, warm pink and gold glow. The trip from Spain, which included a short stop for refuelling, has been silent.

Santiago is sitting next to me, working on his laptop with furious concentration.

I've been trying my best to ignore him, staring out of the window at the country below us instead and pretending he's someone else. Anyone else. But, of course, it's impossible to pretend he's anyone other than who he is, and I hate it.

I hate how he takes up all the room in the helicopter, not to mention all the air, simply by existing. His intense, kinetic presence makes me feel as if I'm sharing space with a live wire that sparks and crackles, electrocuting everything it comes into contact with.

He's electrocuting me by sitting so close, the seats positioned side by side with no space between them.

The trip has taken a couple of hours, which has made me hyper-aware of him. Of the way his powerful body fills the seat, his long legs outstretched. Of his long, blunt fingers and how they move on the laptop keys, fast and light. Of his scent and how it makes my mouth water, and me wonder how a scent so warm can match a man so apparently cold, hard and arrogant.

Except, while he might be hard and arrogant, he's certainly not cold and I know that all too well. He proved exactly how hot he was four months ago in the church, and now that knowledge has imprinted itself on my brain. He was a volcano, a fever, a desert sun, burning and burning, and setting me alight with him. I hate him for that.

I hate that I couldn't pretend I didn't want him.

I hate that I made that promise to him.

When he offered his 'services' in my bed, at first I couldn't believe his audacity. I don't have any issue with sex workers, but I'm not one and his casual assumption that I was at first shocked me, then enraged me. And *then* to assume that I'd as easily sleep with him as his father...

Not that I have any right to be enraged about that, when of course I *did* sleep with him—or, rather, I had sex with him, which is the whole reason I'm in this mess to start with.

The worst part of that scene back at the hacienda, though, was that I still wanted him and couldn't hide it from him. When he touched me I should have pulled away, but I didn't. It was as if his hand gripping my jaw kept me pinned, even though there was no strength in it. That and the look in his obsidian eyes…so much heat and hunger.

My skin went tight the moment he touched me, every part of my body aching. It wanted him and couldn't see anything wrong with his offer, but there was no way *I* could accept it, no matter what my body thought.

Sleeping with him again would be yet another mistake and I've made so many already. I don't want to get the paternity test he demanded, either, for fear of him taking the child away from me once he knows the results. And I certainly didn't want to go to Paris with him.

Sadly for me, he's been inexplicably adamant about the test, and then he countered my demand for his word that he'd let me keep the baby with a demand of his own: if I wanted to stay with my child, I would have to be in his bed.

A shiver works its way through me at the thought, and I have a horrible feeling that it's not fear but anticipation.

He wants me, he's made no secret of it, and the needy part of me loves that he does, even if he quite clearly hates that he does. That part of me *wants* to be in his bed, wants his touch, wants him inside me, because it's desperate for the pleasure he can give me. It's been starved of it for too long, and that moment in the church alcove wasn't enough, not nearly enough.

I shouldn't have agreed to promise him my body, but I couldn't see a way out of the trap he'd laid.

Sure, tell yourself he forced you into a corner. If you truly hadn't wanted him, you wouldn't have said yes.

I stare sightlessly out of the helicopter as we fly over the city, the truth settling down inside me. I might have lied to him, but I can't lie to myself. I *do* want him. When he made me the same offer eighteen months ago, even though I refused, I couldn't stop thinking about what it would have been like if I'd said yes. If I'd been with him instead of his father.

You know what it would have been like.

I do. It would have been incredible and that's what I was afraid of. Even now, the thought of being in his bed, of getting another chance with him, thrills me down to the bone. And I hate that too.

He shifts in the seat beside me, settling back, his elbow on the armrest close to mine. His attention is on his laptop screen, focused and intent, his black brows drawn together.

I don't know why he wants this baby so badly. I don't know much about him at all, in fact, and that was deliberate on my part. After that night at the fundraiser, when I saw him at the bar, I knew he would be my ruin, and ever since then I've avoided the temptation of finding out more about him.

Antonio had nothing but venom to spit when he talked about him, calling his son 'difficult' and 'cold' and a 'traitor'. He'd tell me that Santiago had his mother's 'emotional weaknesses', though he didn't go into details and I didn't ask. I didn't want to know and I still don't.

But…maybe I should know. Maybe I should find out

more about him, especially since he's the father of my baby, and will be in my future one way or another. I do know one thing though: if he's as full of hate with our child as he is with me, I won't stand for it. I just won't. I want our child to be loved and wanted, because I know what it means to be unloved and unwanted. I know it all too well.

After years of being bounced from one foster family to another, I was placed with that wonderful family, along with another girl. I was thirteen and she was ten. Our foster parents were amazing, were everything we both wanted, warm and loving and patient. They made me feel, for the first time in my life, as if I had value, as if I had finally found a home.

At least they did until they adopted the ten-year-old, Lisa, and not me. I was placed with another family, while Lisa got to stay with them. There were no explanations given for why they didn't want me. I was left to work out what went wrong on my own, but I was never able to figure out a reason. Was I too angry? Too disobedient? Too stubborn? Or was it that I was too needy? Too clingy? Too old?

No one ever said, and I never got another chance at adoption again. After I'd aged out of the system, I was left on my own. I've been on my own ever since, but I've come to terms with that. Being alone is safer anyway, because when it comes down to it, the only person you can ever rely on is yourself. Other people will let you down if given half a chance, so I make sure to never give them a chance.

You're giving him *a chance by trusting him not to take the baby away.*

I don't trust him. I trust his word, that's all. And if he betrays that trust? I'll fight him with everything I have.

The helicopter lands on a helipad in the inner city, and from there Santiago whisks me into a car that takes us through Paris's ancient, winding streets. Fifteen minutes later the car turns into the gated courtyard of a magnificent old mansion with a walled garden. Once we're parked we get out, and Santiago ushers me into the house.

It's breathtakingly beautiful inside. The golden-brown parquet floors have been worn by the constant tread of people over hundreds of years, and there's a beautiful staircase that curves elegantly up to the second floor. Chandeliers sparkle with light from the setting sun, casting glitters of pink and gold along the white walls, the same colours echoing in the silken rugs that cover the floors.

Santiago leaves me in the care of a housekeeper, whom he introduces as Helene, who then shows me into a pretty sitting room that looks over the garden outside. It's so peaceful-looking, you'd never know you were in the middle of a city. There are pots full of flowers and herbs, and green lawns and hedges, plus an elegant pond with a fountain, as well as a couple of large oaks.

The sitting room itself has white walls, with gilded moulding around the doors and windows. The furniture, too, is delicate and white, with pops of gilt and gold in the cushions scattered on the sofa and window seat. It feels almost feminine and a strange decor choice for a man like Santiago, who is so very…masculine in all ways.

After a moment or two of looking around, I sit down on the cushioned and very pleasant window seat and prepare myself. I'm going to need every ounce of will I possess to face what's to come, both from the results of this test and from my promise to him.

A shiver whispers over my skin, my body already softening at the thought of being in his bed, the ache between my legs deepening. It's been four months since those frantic moments with him in the church, and, as much as I'm loath to admit it to myself, I've been dreaming about them. Thinking about them. Going over and over them as I lie in my lonely bed at night, and it *is* lonely. Antonio and I slept in separate beds, because he had health issues that required him getting up in the middle of the night, and he didn't want to disturb me. I was more than happy with that, since I didn't want to be disturbed either. I never felt lonely in my bed before Santiago, but I felt it in those months after Antonio's funeral, and it galls me that, even now, all I can think about is him.

Perhaps he's right, though. Perhaps a physical affair with him is what we need to finally get each other out of our systems.

And then where will you be?

I push the thought away. I can't think about that now. What I have to get through first is him finding out that he really is the father of my baby, and what demands he'll make of me. Because if there's one thing I *do* know about Santiago Veracruz, it's that he *will* make demands. In which case I need to have a response ready.

I've only been sitting here for five minutes when the door opens and Santiago strides in, followed by another man carrying a small medical bag.

I steel myself, my hands gripped tightly together in my lap.

Santiago's black gaze finds mine instantly. 'This is Dr Dubois,' he says, gesturing at the man. 'He's already done a cheek swab for me. Now it's your turn to provide a blood sample.'

I nod, giving the doctor a polite smile as he comes over to the window seat and takes some equipment from his bag. Within a few minutes he takes a sample of my blood, and once that's done he says something in French to Santiago, who nods. Then the doctor leaves the room.

'The results will be available in a couple of hours.' Santiago's black stare pins me to the window seat. 'I have my own lab and assistants, naturally.'

Of course he does. Not that I'd expect anything less.

Once again, though, the room feels too small with him in it and more than anything it's making me want to escape. To run out of the door and lose myself in the streets of Paris, far away from his maddening, demanding, inciting presence. But that would be letting him win, and I can't give him the satisfaction. I won't. Besides, even if I did run, he'd probably track me down and find me, and anyway, I have a baby to think of now. We'll be a family, my child and I. The family I used to dream about having during those long, lonely years in foster care, yet never had. And this time I'll be the one choosing who gets to be in that family. I will never have to suffer not being chosen again.

So instead of running, I make a show of sitting here calmly, ready for any eventuality. 'So, what would you like to do while we wait?' I ask. 'Shall I take my clothes off for you now or later?'

CHAPTER EIGHT

Santiago

SHE'S THE VERY picture of self-possession as she sits in the window seat, so very cool, so very calm. The sunset casts rays of pink and orange light through the window, making her hair gleam like spun gold as it falls over her shoulders and making her skin seem almost pearlescent. She looks like a stained-glass window, glowing with colour and light.

I want to tell her that yes, she should take her clothes off for me right now, but, since she's expecting me to say that, I won't. I can't have her be so calm, not when I'm pushed to the limit.

The trip from Spain was long, and Beatrix sitting next to me in the helicopter the whole time was unbearable. She said nothing, while I tried to concentrate on a research report—'tried' being the operative word.

Science has always been my escape, where logic and facts rule. It's real, tangible, and when I'm working on my research, nothing else matters. But I couldn't concentrate on the report, no matter how hard I tried, because she was right there. Smelling of flowers, her body radiating the kind of soft, feminine heat that I find utterly irresistible. Every so often I'd find myself glancing at her, studying her undeniably beautiful face, wondering what was going on in that pretty head of hers, which is something I almost never think about, since I don't care what goes on in other people's heads. It's what they do that matters to me more than what they think.

But not with her. It's maddening. I don't understand why she's different, since it's not something I've ever thought about with any of my other lovers.

Perhaps it's because she'll be the mother of my child, and I need to know what kind of mother she'll be. Money is important to her—that's why she married my father—and I could assume she'll be just as mercenary about motherhood. Then again, she was adamant that she wanted to keep the baby, going so far as to extract a promise that I wouldn't take it away from her, so it's clear she feels very strongly about it.

I admire that strength of feeling in her, as much as I hate to admit it. A mother *should* feel strongly about her child. Parents in general should put their child first, regardless of their own wants and needs. I'm not here for anyone's selfishness, not after my own upbringing, and my father's masterclass in being a self-centred bastard is not something I'm going to emulate.

Yet how I'm going to raise my own child once it's born is a question I'll have to think about later, once the results of the test come back and I have all the facts at hand. For now, I have my father's widow to manage.

She's waiting for me to reply, her hands clasped in her lap, the very picture of serenity. But she's not as serene as she likes to make out, not when her knuckles are so white.

My temper prowls, provoked by her apparent calm and sarcastic tone, so I don't reply immediately, studying her instead, watching as the colour floods into her cheeks. 'No, thank you,' I say eventually, mimicking what she said about touching me back in Spain. 'Perhaps later.'

Her gaze flickers and I feel a brief surge of triumph. Was she truly hoping I'd ask her to do that? How satisfying not to oblige her.

This petty war you have with her is pointless. What do you hope to accomplish by it? She lost her husband, she's pregnant, and you've dragged her all the way to Paris purely for spite's sake.

The thought comes without warning, a reminder from my largely atrophied conscience, and I have to turn abruptly away so she doesn't see it, striding over to the mantelpiece instead.

I don't normally regret my decisions. The only one I've ever regretted is the choice I made to tell my mother about my father's affairs. Considering the consequences of that choice both for her and me, I may have chosen differently if I'd spent more time thinking about it and less time being furious at my father for lying.

Since then, though, I've never let my emotions dictate my choices. I've always made them logically and after due consideration of the facts, and that's why I brought Beatrix here to Paris.

I didn't trust her word about the blood test, because she's lied to me before, and I couldn't leave her to complete it herself for that reason. And as for her grief over my father, I saw her eyes at the funeral. They were dry.

That comment was petty, though, and needlessly cruel.

I stare down at the ornate carriage clock on the mantelpiece. It's one of my mother's favourite pieces. I bought it for her when I got my first decent pay cheque after working in a lab in Madrid. I had this room decorated just for her, but she's never been in it. She's still in the rehab facility in Switzerland. I haven't told her anything about the child, or about Beatrix, and I won't. Not until she's well enough to bear it, though I suspect she never will be.

Which is your fault.

No, none of that was *my* fault. She was the one who chose to heal her broken heart by drinking…no one forced her. Besides, I was only a child at the time, and she wouldn't listen to me when I told her to stop. I even hid the gin bottles she kept buying, but she would always find them. So why should I feel guilty? I don't. And looking after her now isn't about guilt, it's about duty.

It's true, though. I *was* being petty. I wanted to get at Beatrix because she gets at me, but that's hardly a reason to be cruel for the sake of it. Also, I can't forget that she's pregnant. I've given no thought to how she might be feeling, pregnant and alone after my father's death. And that *is* my fault. While I'm gifted in physics and mathematics, I'm very bad when it comes to understanding other people's feelings. I have to work at it. Which means that, since her pregnancy is my responsibility, I should be working on understanding hers.

Restlessly, I pick up a small black figurine of a cat then put it down again. Apologies are difficult for me, since I'm wrong so rarely, and I'm finding it difficult now. 'Do you need anything?' I force myself to ask, trying to be conciliatory. 'Some tea? Or perhaps something to eat?'

'Do you really care what I need?' Her voice behind me is cool. 'After all, that didn't seem to bother you when you dragged me away from the hacienda.'

Weren't you supposed to be different from your father?

I grit my teeth. I am *not* him. Yes, I'm used to getting my way and yes, I don't give the needs of others much consideration, but she should be the exception. She's pregnant with my child, therefore her physical needs are important to the health of that child.

I turn around and meet her cool stare. 'The health of my child is dependent on you, so yes, I care.'

This time there is no flickering in her gaze. She holds mine steadily and without flinching. 'You care about the child, then? Interesting.'

A burst of defensive anger fills me, though I thrust it aside. It's that biological imperative again, the primitive in me wanting to defend my ability to care, protect and defend my child.

'Why should that be interesting?' I ask, keeping my tone very neutral.

'Because you seem to care very little for anything or anyone but yourself,' she says, as if she hasn't just fired a harpoon at me. As if the sharp barbs haven't pierced the plates of my armour and sunk deep into my flesh.

However, she doesn't know the vulnerability she's just uncovered and I'm not going to show it to her. It'll only give her more ammunition to use against me, so I thrust the anger away.

'You would be wrong,' I inform her coldly. 'The health of my child is of the utmost importance.'

I move from the mantelpiece, pacing back over to the window seat where she's sitting, only slightly appeased by the slight widening of her eyes at my approach.

I have to remember that. I have to remember that she's not as cool and calm as she looks, that she's just as much at the mercy of our chemistry as I am, and maybe it's time to remind her.

Weren't you not *going to do what she expects?*

I wasn't. But now I'm thinking *why not?* instead.

'Perhaps you'd rather take your clothes off.' I fold my arms and stare down at her. 'I wouldn't object, of course.'

She doesn't seem to find me staring a problem, her gaze steady. 'Make up your mind, *Mr* Veracruz,' she says, again with that tart emphasis on my title. 'You wanted me in your bed; that was what you said. I'd just like to know when that will occur, so I can prepare myself.'

I need to stop reacting to her, yet I can't help myself. The cool challenge in the words slides under my skin, testing my already limited patience and my fraying temper. 'Tell me, how exactly will you prepare yourself?' I counter. 'Will you lie there like a virgin sacrifice, thinking only of England?'

'Too late for that,' she says. 'I'm no longer a virgin, thanks to you.'

For a second the statement sits between us, sharp-edged and bright, but I'm still wrestling with my temper to fully process it. Then I do, and surprise yawns wide inside me.

'You were a virgin?' I demand, trying to think back to that moment in the church, and whether she'd given me any inkling that she was still an innocent. I hadn't given her previous sexual experience much thought at all, admittedly, though she was very clear she'd been with my father.

I'd think this another of her lies if not for the sudden and bright flush of colour blooming in her cheeks. 'I mean, I didn't—'

'Don't lie to me,' I interrupt, holding on to my temper by the skin of my teeth. 'Were you?'

Her pretty mouth tightens. 'What does it matter to you?'

It shouldn't. Virginity is a social construct that I should have no interest in, yet the primitive beast in me disagrees. It wants to be her first, her only.

'I see. So you were, then,' I say flatly, because if she wasn't, she would have said so straight out. 'Why the lies? Are you protecting my father or yourself?'

She's still flushed, sparks of anger glittering in her eyes. She's probably angry that she betrayed herself, but it's too late for that now.

'You assumed.' Her chin lifts. 'And I saw no reason to challenge your assumptions, since you seem so wedded to them.'

You did assume. And you know what they say about assumptions...

My temper heats, yet it's myself I'm angry with. I'm not even sure why, because she's right. I shouldn't care about her virginity, not one iota. And yet...

You don't like the way she sees right through you.

No, I don't.

'What about the lies concerning the baby?' I demand. 'Is anything that comes out of your mouth the truth?'

'I wouldn't have to lie if you weren't such a complete bastard,' she says hotly. The brilliant sapphire blue of her eyes glitters with temper, and in the air around us tension gathers, crackling and sparking. As ever, it's fuelled by our mutual antipathy, and it pulls tighter and tighter, making it difficult for me to concentrate on anything else.

If I want to get anything real out of her, this tension needs to be gone. We need to sate it, and now, before we deal with anything else.

So I take another step towards the window seat, intruding on her personal space, my trousers brushing her knees. And all of a sudden the burning blue flame in her eyes darkens, flickering into violet.

'If I'm such a complete bastard,' I say in a low voice, 'why do you want me so badly?'

Her pale throat moves as she swallows, her attention dropping to my mouth and back up again. 'I don't,' she murmurs, and it sounds like a plea.

'Prove it to me, then.' I reach down, taking a handful of the fabric of her dress and slowly gathering it in my fist. 'Tell me you don't want me to touch you. Tell me that you're not desperate for me. That you don't crave me inside you.' I pull more fabric up, baring her knees. 'Tell me and make me believe it.'

CHAPTER NINE

Beatrix

MY BREATH LODGES in my throat as Santiago gathers my dress slowly in his fist, his black gaze burning into mine. It's all challenge, all fire, making my heartbeat race and the ache between my thighs intensify.

I shouldn't let him get to me the way he does. I shouldn't let him needle me, but he trapped me in my lie about my virginity, and now I'm furious. Both with myself for being so susceptible, and with him for being so awful and yet so bloody hot at the same time.

Perhaps you shouldn't have let yourself soften when he asked you if you needed something to eat.

I wish I could deny that, but I can't. For a second, I actually thought he was being conciliatory, but when he turned around I could see he was forcing it. That he didn't actually care. He was only concerned with the health of his 'incubator'.

Which shouldn't matter to me. I shouldn't care about my importance to him or otherwise, since he's right about one thing: the health and wellbeing of our child is what truly matters. Yet, to my continued fury, there's a part of me that does want more, that wants to matter to someone in some way, though why I'm fixating on him, I have no idea.

Now, though, what I know is that I can't allow him to take charge of this. He did so in the church, and I got so lost in what he did to me that I didn't even realise we hadn't used protection. I can't afford to get so lost again.

I'm alone and pregnant, and in his house, and I need to take back some of the power I left behind when he dragged me here.

I need to be the one who undoes him, rather than the other way around, so, while I'd love to prove to him that I don't want him, I won't. Because it's not true and we both know it. The time for lies is over. Now it's time for me to embrace the truth and ruin him with it.

So I look up at him, into his hot black eyes, and at the same time I pull my dress out of his fingers. 'You want to know what I really want?' I ask. 'I'll show you.'

I put my hands on his strong thighs and push him back slightly to give myself room. Then I slide from the window seat, and go down on my knees on the pale carpet.

His breath catches, I hear it, and when I look up at him I see that his midnight gaze is full of flames. He's not bothering to hide how he wants me, and the needy part of me glories in it, even as a deeper part is afraid of it. Afraid I can't trust it. Because I've thought people wanted me before, and have been proven wrong, and I can't go through that again. I won't.

Except a man's sexual desire is difficult to hide, and I can trust that if nothing else. Though this isn't about his desire for me. This is about my desire for him, and, since he's demanded the truth, I'll give it. But in doing so I'll wreck him the way he wrecked me, and that's only fair.

I lift my hands to his belt and begin to undo it, and he doesn't say a word. He lets me open the buckle, then the button of his trousers, and then I'm drawing down the zip of his fly. He's already hard, the outline of his cock pressing against the black fabric of his boxers, and the sheer size of him makes my mouth dry. It also sends a fierce burst of satisfaction through me, that I've made him this hard and so quickly, just by kneeling for him.

I reach for him, drawing him out then looking up into his face, wanting to see the effect my touch has on him.

His expression is ferocious with hunger, his skin drawn tight over the exquisite bone structure of his face, and his eyes are like cut jet, glittering and dark. He's powerful like this, towering over me at his feet, yet that power is an illusion.

I'm the one with the true power as I run my fingers over his hot, velvety skin, watching the pleasure flare in his eyes. I wonder if he knows, and whether he cares, but then his fingers thread into my hair, his touch almost gentle, and the triumph in me wavers as my own hunger rises in response.

You're playing with fire. You need to be careful.

I know this, yet the thought is a dim one. Reality is

the hard length of him in my hands, and the guttural sound he makes as I lean forward to take him in my mouth. It's the salty, masculine taste of him as I draw him deeper, and the way he reaches for me, his fingers curling in my hair and gripping me tightly.

'You're hungry for me, aren't you?' His dark voice is low and rough, his Spanish accent pronounced. 'So desperate to have me in your mouth.'

I nod again, giving him the truth, because my sexuality is power. It's the power I had over his father, and it's the power I'll have over him, too. It's the only power I have. And I have no compunction in using it.

He wanted you first. All this time he wanted you. That's why he's so angry with you.

He did want me, but I didn't choose him, and there's a reason for that. I need to remember that reason now, because it would be so easy to lose myself in him. To get lost in his taste and his touch, and the glory of his own hunger for me. Antonio wanted me, but I could have been any pretty woman to him, it didn't need to be me. But Santiago didn't want any other pretty woman, he wanted *me*. And that feels good. Too good.

'That's it,' he purrs, his voice deepening even further as I run my tongue along his length, use my teeth against his skin. 'Take all of me like a good girl.'

And I do. I want to. I want to be his good girl, to taste him, take him, rip a growl from his throat the way I did back in the church. I want to watch him come apart, and all because of me.

'Yes,' he murmurs as I swallow him deeper and his hips move, thrusting into my mouth. 'This is the truth of you, isn't it? Kneeling at my feet, with my cock in your mouth. That's what you want, what you've always wanted.'

The words should make me feel small and belittled. Yet the way he says them, with the rasp of pleasure catching at all the vowels and consonants, I don't feel either small or belittled. *I* put that pleasure in his voice and he *likes* me kneeling at his feet. If that's the truth of me, it's also the truth of him, because not only does he like it, he also wants it. It's what *he's* always wanted, too.

This truth is both of ours. We're in it together, so when I look up into his eyes and see the pleasure I'm giving him reflected there I feel strong. I feel powerful. And more than anything, I feel wanted.

So I take as much of him as I can, unable to tear my gaze away from him. Watching him come undone as his grip on my hair firms, the movements of his hips jerky and hurried. And when he finally comes he doesn't look away, letting me see the orgasm overwhelming him, his handsome face tightening, his mouth drawn in a snarl as he mutters something savage in Spanish.

Afterwards I lean my cheek against his thigh, the wool of his trousers prickling against my skin. My heartbeat is thundering. I can taste the salt of him in my mouth and I'm so turned on, I'm desperate. But this isn't about my pleasure. This is me undoing him for a change, and not vice versa.

His grip on my hair eases, his fingers moving with gentleness, and a spike of longing hits me, so intense that I have to close my eyes as tears prickle at the inside of my lids. I should pull away, get to my feet, put some distance between us again, yet I can't bring myself to move. I've never been touched like this before, with gentleness, almost with tenderness, and it's undoing me even as the pleasure I gave undid him.

Antonio never touched me like this. My pleasure didn't concern him, only the pleasure he received from me, and he never held me afterwards. I've never had anyone else touch me like this, either. Not since I was thirteen, when I used to get hugs from the foster parents who eventually ended up adopting Lisa, not me.

I once read that humans can die from lack of touch, and, with Santiago's hand in my hair and the way my whole body responds to his light caress, I can believe it.

All too soon, though, he steps away and I hear him zip up his fly. This time I don't look up, painfully conscious that I'm kneeling at his feet, and that the moment of unexpected vulnerability has made my newly acquired power feel as if it's slipping through my fingers. I have to be strong. I have to be invulnerable. I can never let him see what his gentle touch did to me.

Yet before I can find my usual calm he slides a finger beneath my chin, tilting my head up, and his gaze meets mine. I'm expecting to see the normal hate, so I'm thrown off-balance when I see that his dark brows are drawn together in a frown, and there's no anger in his midnight eyes, only puzzlement.

I try to pull away, not wanting him to see my weakness, but he anticipates it and his grip on my chin tightens.

'Don't,' I whisper, unable to stop myself.

He doesn't let go. 'Why were you crying?'

Oh, God. He saw.

I attempt to pull away again, desperate to protect myself, but his grip is unbreakable.

'Did I do that?' he demands. 'Did I make you cry?'

I blink the remaining tears away hard. 'Why do you keep asking me questions?' I can't quite hide the shake in my voice. 'Why do you even care?'

His gaze flickers and quite suddenly he takes his finger away.

I'm just catching my breath and armouring myself once again, when his hands settle under my elbows and he pulls me to my feet, and this time he doesn't let go.

A startled breath escapes me, my heartbeat continuing to thud in my head. His hands are warm, his grip gentle, yet his gaze burns, demanding things once again.

'I don't want to make you cry,' he says forcefully. 'I don't want to hurt you.'

'If you don't want to hurt me,' I snap, 'then maybe you should stop being such a prick to me.'

It's too late to pretend that he doesn't affect me or that I'm not hurt by the things he says, or by his anger. Too late to pretend to myself that his opinion of me doesn't matter. Far, far too late.

Maybe it's the pregnancy hormones, but it's not that I care about him per se, it's more that he's just one more person who hates me, and I can't bear it. I don't have the bandwidth for it, not any more.

Defensive fury rises in his eyes in response, and I

brace myself for whatever horrible thing he's going to say. But just as my muscles tighten his fury flickers and dies, leaving behind it puzzlement again, and something else. Something that looks a lot like regret.

'I… I'm sorry.' He releases me and takes a step back, his expression shuttered. 'I'll send Helene in. Please let her know if there's anything you need, anything at all.'

Then, without another word, he turns and leaves the room.

CHAPTER TEN

Santiago

I'M IN MY ground-floor study with the view of the garden and fountain, listening to my mother's voice down the phone as she tells me about her day. This is a daily occurrence, and it's reassuring to hear her voice, especially when the doctors' reports of her progress are less so. She's not doing too badly, all things considered, but she's not well enough to come to Paris yet.

Maybe that's for the best, especially in regard to the situation I have here at present, which is not settled in any way, shape or form.

'How are you, darling boy?' she asks. 'Have you found a wife yet?'

My mother is always more affectionate in the evenings after her meds—it's not about me personally, it never is—and she regards me finding a wife as the thing that will finally 'fix me'. And yes, she uses those words. She's always thought I was broken in some way. It's the only thing she and my father ever agreed on.

'No,' I tell her as patiently as I can. 'That's not a priority right now and you know that.'

She sighs as if I'm the world's biggest disappointment, which I'm sure is true, no matter how big my company gets or how much money I make. She views my interest in science with abhorrence, and has never understood it or me.

'You should make it a priority,' she says with dogged determination. 'You need a wife, Santiago. Trust me on this.'

I don't know why I'd trust her when her own marriage ended so appallingly, and she ended up being so burned by it. She has a very selective memory about some things.

I should tell her that she should stop trying to fix me, that I'm not broken, but I've told her that before and she never listens. She only gets hurt and tells me I'm being mean to her. Mean to her like Antonio was mean to her.

'Yes, Mother.' It's the only thing I can say to her these days. 'I'll call you tomorrow evening, okay?'

I put the phone down, then check my watch. The results of the paternity test should be available any time now, not that I'm at all worried about the results. Not after Beatrix finally stopped lying to me.

I lace my hands behind my head and lean back in my chair, staring up at the ceiling, going over what happened between us an hour ago.

Her, telling me that she was a virgin before our encounter in the church.

Her, on her knees, giving me the most intense pleasure I've ever experienced.

Her, looking up at me with tears in her eyes, real pain shining there in a moment of vulnerability.

She finally gave me the truth, and I should be feeling satisfied about it. I should be feeling triumphant that I managed to force it from her. Certainly when she went down on her knees, pleasure was all I could think about. And how I liked seeing her kneeling. How much I wanted her to take me in her mouth.

Then she did and she wasn't cold or calm, or serene. No, she looked up at me, her cheeks flushed, as if she couldn't bear to look away, and I didn't want her to. I wanted her to see the pleasure she was giving me.

But it was in the aftermath, when she put her cheek against my thigh, that I found my fingers idly caressing the soft silk of her hair, simply enjoying the feel of it against my skin. Enjoying, too, the trusting way she leaned against me, and it…did something to me. Hollowed me out in a way I wasn't expecting, and couldn't articulate.

In that moment I needed to see the expression on her face, so I caught her beneath the chin, and tilted her head up. Only to find her blue eyes liquid with unshed tears.

It shocked me, those tears, and even now as I think about them, I'm still shocked.

Why shocked? She's pregnant with your child and you've been nothing but awful to her.

That conscience of mine keeps on nagging me, and

I don't like it. I've never been bothered by it before, so I don't know why now it keeps sliding the knife in.

I shove myself out of my chair, and pace to the bookshelves, staring sightlessly at the spines, my body full of a strange restless energy. As if I want to physically outrun the whispers in my head. The whispers that keep telling me that I've behaved appallingly to a woman who did nothing wrong except *not* choose me. That no matter how many logical arguments I give myself, I'm letting my own sexual jealousy get to me.

You made her cry.

I put my hands on the bookshelves and lean on them, looking down at the carpet, as a thread of cold shame winds through me. I had no idea I could be so affected by a woman's tears. By *anyone's* tears, for that matter. My mother used to cry frequently—still does—and her tears used to hurt when I was a boy. I hated that she was in pain, and after my father threw us out I'd do anything I could to make her stop crying. But that was before she made it clear that there was nothing I could do to make her feel better. Nothing I could do to heal her pain. I was the reason she was hurt, the reason we were thrown out of our home, and she didn't want anything at all from me, most especially not being told to stop drinking.

That she didn't want anything from me was, of course, a lie. She wanted the money I earned for her and the attention I gave her, and she took it all, even as she made sure that I never forgot why she drank and why she had so many difficulties with depression. It was my fault. Everything was my fault.

But I refused to feel guilt for that, just as I hardened my heart against her tears, made sure they didn't affect me.

That should include the tears of pretty Beatrix. Yet I can't stop seeing the gleam of them in her eyes as she knelt at my feet. Can't stop hearing the catch in her voice when she told me that if I didn't want to hurt her, I shouldn't be such a prick to her.

She's a passionate woman, this I know. Both her anger and her desire burn hot, no matter how cold she appears, so it stands to reason that she should also feel hurt just as powerfully. She's more vulnerable than she appears, especially now, pregnant with my child.

You let your anger control you when it comes to her.

My jaw tightens as the unpleasant truth hits home. As much as I don't want to admit it, I do let it control me. *I'm* supposed to be the cool one, the logical one, yet she makes me feel anything but cool and logical, and I can't stand it. It makes me want to needle her, ruffle her, disturb her the way she disturbs me.

That's a poor reason to be cruel to someone.

It is. Not to mention selfish, and I pride myself on not being selfish.

My phone vibrates in my pocket, and I push myself away from the bookcase, pulling it out and looking down at the screen. It's the lab. The results are back. There's an email in my inbox, with an attachment, and the test results are clear: I'm the father of the child with a ninety-nine per cent accuracy.

This shouldn't come as a surprise, since that's exactly what I'm expecting, yet I'm also aware of that powerful feeling coursing through me once again, all primitive, possessive satisfaction and an almost heady triumph.

I loathe it. It's ridiculous to feel this way simply because I've done what nearly the entire population of the globe has done, which is to perpetuate the species. It's not different. It's not special. It's what I was biologically engineered to do. Yet for some reason, I want to shout my accomplishment from the rooftops as if no one in human history has ever done this before.

With some difficulty I force the feeling away, and grip tight to my logic. Now I have all the facts, I need to be measured about this, because I have some decisions to make. The child is mine, and, while I've never wanted children, I will have one all the same and I need to decide how to manage that.

Naturally, I'll be nothing like my own father, putting himself and what he wanted above everything, even his own child. I will never throw him or her away as if they were garbage lying around that has to be got rid of. They will live with me. And as for Beatrix, well, that is something we'll need to discuss.

I put my phone back in my pocket, and stride out of the office to find my housekeeper. Helene tells me that she put Beatrix on the terrace in the garden with some tea and pastries, since 'the poor woman looked dead on her feet'.

Once again a feeling of shame grips me, and none of the defensive arguments I made to myself about how I did offer her something to eat make any difference. I dragged her here, made her give a blood sample, forced the issue of our chemistry, then I put her on her knees to give me pleasure, only then to make her cry. Those are not the actions of an unselfish man.

Perhaps you're more like your father than you thought.

I grit my teeth, and shove the snide whisper away as I find my way to the stone terrace outside at the back of the house.

It's one of my mother's favourite places to sit, since it's very peaceful, with the flowers and lawn, and pond with a fountain that fills the air with the musical sound of running water.

Beatrix is sitting on one of the cushioned chairs at the delicate wrought-iron outdoor table. She's holding a cup of steaming tea between her hands, looking down into the cup as if she's trying to divine her future. The sun has gone down, the last rays lighting the sky above her and outlining the soft curve of her cheek in gold, her loose hair a wavy silken waterfall.

She's stunningly beautiful sitting there in the sunset, and I can feel my hunger for her rise yet again, even as the feeling of shame at how I've treated her tightens still further.

She raises her head at my approach, and I catch the flicker of anxiety in her blue eyes before it vanishes. And in a moment of sudden clarity I realise that her anxiety is because of me. Because she's afraid of what I might do, of what I might ask of her, and she has reason to be afraid. Especially considering what I've already done.

'Don't tell me,' she says before I can speak. 'You're the father.'

'Yes.' I move over to the table and sit down opposite her.

She lifts one golden brow, still trying to hold on to her ice-queen mask. 'What? No snide comments about what a liar I am? Not even a gloat about how you did what your father couldn't?'

She's angry still, and I don't blame her for it.

Apologies are difficult, yet I can make them when I know I've been in the wrong, and I can admit that I am in the wrong here.

'I'm sorry, Beatrix,' I offer, because she deserves this at least from me. 'I'm sorry for my behaviour towards you earlier. It was unconscionable.'

She blinks, surprise crossing her face. 'You're sorry? Seriously?'

'I'm never anything but serious,' I tell her. 'I meant what I said, that I didn't want to hurt you, that I didn't want to make you cry. And I'm sorry I did both.'

She blinks again, a fleeting look of bewilderment crossing her face. 'What brought this on?'

I don't want to explain myself, but I make myself do it, because, once again, she deserves this from me. 'I have…reflected on my actions,' I say slowly. 'And realise that I haven't been fair to you.'

Her gaze narrows. 'I see. If I'd known all you needed was a blow job to be nice to me, I would have given you one earlier.'

I'm irritated she would think *that* had anything to do with it, but, considering I didn't reflect on my behaviour until after that had happened, she has a right to question me. 'It wasn't the blow job,' I say. 'It was your tears.'

She stares at me a second, shock in her eyes, then abruptly glances down at her teacup and the fragrant, steaming liquid in it. 'If you're expecting me to apologise in return,' she says after a moment, 'then I'm afraid you'll be waiting until hell freezes over.'

'Why would you apologise?' I ask. 'You did nothing wrong.'

She keeps her gaze on her cup. 'And yet you keep punishing me.'

My muscles are tight, my jaw aching. Because as much as I don't want to, I have to acknowledge this truth too, that I *have* been punishing her, and for the most childish of reasons: she chose *him*, not me.

'I apologise for that also,' I say stiffly. 'That was wrong of me.'

She doesn't respond, and a silence falls, heavy, weighted.

I don't like the quality of that silence, how it gets under my skin and stays there, making me think of all the things I've done to her, all the things I've thought about her, and how wrong they were, and I don't like it. Especially when we have other, more important things to discuss.

'As to the baby,' I say finally, into the quiet, 'now I have all the facts, I can make a decision about it.'

She looks up at that. '*We*,' she says, blue eyes full of determination. '*We* will make a decision.'

CHAPTER ELEVEN

Beatrix

SANTIAGO'S BLACK GAZE is direct, his expression granite hard. Sitting across from me in his exquisite dark blue suit, with his hard stare and his handsome features, he's like a wall of immovable, masculine stone. A wall I want to take a sledgehammer to and break down.

After he left me in the sitting room, I didn't know quite what to do. His sudden change of mood from fury to controlled politeness was bewildering. He said he didn't want to hurt me, but he didn't actually mean that, I know he didn't. It's never stopped him before, after all. He never seemed to be a man moved by tears, either.

Not long after he'd gone, Helene entered the room, smiling at me and telling me in English that I looked as if I needed to sit down and rest with some hot tea and a pastry or two.

Her kindness was a balm to my wounded soul, and so I let her mother and fuss around me as she sat me in the beautiful garden, then brought me tea and the pastries she'd mentioned.

I hadn't realised how much I needed both until after I'd had a few sips of tea and a couple of bites of a pastry. The tea and food at least revived me enough to prepare myself for the return of the test results and whatever 'decision' Santiago was going to make.

I'd braced myself as he strode onto the terrace, bringing with him his usual tense, electric energy, and expecting once again his usual fury. Except it wasn't there. There had been another expression in his dark eyes, and it wasn't until he'd sat down and offered me his apology that I realised the expression was yet again one of regret.

He didn't look away as he'd said the words. He held my gaze the whole time, letting me see that yes, he *was* serious, and that he meant it.

It was the last thing I expected of him, and I honestly had no idea how to take it, especially considering that it was my stupid tears that had prompted it.

I really don't like that he saw me being vulnerable. Even if those tears did cause him to have a change of heart, the fact that he saw them still makes me feel weak, and I'm angry at myself for not being strong enough.

Which doesn't help me now that the truth has been revealed, the truth I already knew, that he *is* the father of my child.

My insides knot and twist with anger and fear, and that nagging, unquenchable desire for the man across from me. A hot, toxic mess of emotion.

He has to know, though, that this is not *his* decision. This is *our* decision, because I refuse to be cut out of my baby's life.

His gaze flickers as if I've scored a hit, but all he says is, 'Yes, of course it's our decision.'

'I'm not leaving my child,' I tell him once again, in no uncertain terms. 'What I would like is to bring them up at the Veracruz estate.'

He stares at me, unblinking for a long moment. Then he sits back in his chair, stretching his long, powerful body out as he folds his arms across his broad chest. 'No,' he says succinctly. 'I live here in Paris and I'm hoping my mother will join me eventually. I would prefer the child to live with me.'

A little shock goes through me. His mother? Antonio never talked about his first wife, not a word. All I knew was that he divorced her years and years before he met me.

'She's here?' I can't help asking.

Something flickers across his face, gone too quickly for me to read. 'Not at present.' His tone darkens, an edge creeping into it. 'But she'll be here at some point, and I'm sure she'd very much like to meet her grandchild.'

Her grandchild. By her late husband's second wife and son.

The situation seems so complex all of a sudden. So convoluted and difficult. I want to be back at the hacienda, where at least there was only myself to manage, and I didn't have to think about Santiago and all the issues associated with him.

But you're not. You're here. He's the father of your child and you're going to have to deal with him one way or the other.

I take a sip of tea to moisten my mouth. 'What exactly is your objection to moving back to Spain?' I ask, trying not to sound confrontational for a change. 'Is it just about your mother?'

His brows lower. 'No. My head office is here and so are my employees.' There's no give in his tone, none at all. 'Also…' he pauses, his eyes glittering '…you made me a promise.'

A flush of heat goes through me. Yes, I did make him a promise. That if he wouldn't take the child from me, I'd be in his bed. Right now, I'd love to break that promise, argue for staying at the Veracruz estate, since it's mine now, and the thought of leaving what I thought would be my home fills me with exhaustion. But he's a man without mercy, and, as he's already made plain, he wants our child to stay with him.

I could fight him on this. I do have the resources. But they're not limitless, and I'll likely run out of money long before he will. It'll be a protracted legal fight, and I really don't want to spend my child's inheritance on fighting with their father. Yet I want a home for them. A place where they feel they belong.

It could be here, in Paris. It wouldn't be the end of the world, yet the idea feels precarious. This isn't *my* home. This isn't *my* place. After so many years to finally have a place of my own, and then to be ripped away from it would be devastating. Staying here will mean I'm the child's mother and Santiago's lover, but nothing else. I'll have no legal right to anything. I'll be back to having no power and no agency, unless…

I blink as an unexpected idea occurs to me. There's one way I could have power here, one way I could legally feel as if this was *my* home, too.

If I was his wife.

Across the table, Santiago's black eyes narrow. 'You've decided something,' he says. 'What is it?'

I meet his gaze, determined to hold it this time. 'I'll keep my promise to you, be in your bed the way you want me to be. But I want some protection for myself in return. Legal protection.'

His frown deepens. 'I can draw up a contract if that's—'

'No,' I interrupt. 'I'm not talking about a contract.'

'Then what are you talking about?'

'I'm talking about being your wife.'

The words hang between us, sharp and bright, and a strange, fizzing excitement moves through me, though I can't think for the life of me why. Like my marriage to his father, it wouldn't be an emotional marriage. It would be more a legal agreement that would provide me with some surety, stability, and protection.

He stares at me, his expression utterly unreadable. 'You want me to marry you?' The question is so determinedly neutral that I'm sure he hates the idea.

But I don't look away. 'Yes. It's what you're essentially wanting from me. I'm only asking to make it legal.'

His black eyes glitter with that familiar mix of heat and anger, but I'm used to that from him. I can do Santiago when he's hungry and furious. That, at least, I know, unlike his apology, which was confusing.

'So you want to add me to your trophy cabinet?' he asks in an edged tone. 'Another Veracruz to add to your list of conquests?'

I fight down my own defensiveness, not taking his bait. 'If you want me to upend the life I've managed to create for myself in Spain, and move to Paris, where I own nothing and have nothing, because you want to stay here, then you'll have to give me some surety that my place here is secure.' I keep my voice calm, cool. Logical. That's something he should appreciate.

A muscle ticks in his jaw. 'You could stay in Spain. No one is forcing you to move.'

'You said you wouldn't take the baby away from me,' I counter. 'You promised.'

'And you promised you'd stay in my bed,' he snaps, his hold on his temper clearly not as good as he wants me to believe.

'Marry me,' I say. 'And I'll be there every night.'

'Why would I need to,' he leans forward as if to emphasise his point, 'when you've already promised me everything?'

I take a breath, trying to batten down the hatches on my sudden, rising panic. I've spent my life trying to find stability, trying to find safety, trying to find a home that no one can take away from me. I thought marrying Antonio would give me that, and it did, only for my own desperate need to undermine everything and upend the little life I'd built for myself. I can't face the idea of doing it again. I'll be at the mercy of Santiago's desire, which will fade soon enough, and then where will I be? And what about my child?

With a supreme effort of will, I force away the panic. Logic, that's what I need. That's what I'll have to use to appeal to him, since playing on his feelings won't work, I know that already. 'What about when this chemistry of ours is dead?' I ask. 'What about when either of us doesn't want the other any more? What if I fall in love with another man and marry him instead, and petition for custody of—'

'You will *not* be marrying another man,' he interrupts with barely suppressed fury. 'Not while you are sleeping with me.'

Something inside me shivers at the possessive note in his voice. The needy part of me, the part that loves being wanted the way he wants me. I don't like giving in to it, but it does remind me that I can use his possessiveness to get what I want, too. That there is one feeling of his that I can play on: his jealousy.

'I'll be faithful as your wife,' I say, my skin tightening as I hold his stark black gaze. 'I believe in marriage vows.'

He says nothing for a long moment, his gaze roaming over my face, studying me as if I'm one of his experiments and it's not going according to his plan. 'My mother won't be pleased if I marry you,' he says at last.

No, I don't suppose she would be. 'Do you care what your mother thinks?'

'Yes,' he says unexpectedly. 'I've cared for her ever since Antonio threw us out.'

Another little shock goes through me. That's something I was never told about. 'He threw you out?'

Santiago's lip curls. 'Surely you must know that.'

'No. He spoke of you, of course, but not about your mother. He never mentioned his first marriage.'

Santiago's eyes narrow into thin slits of obsidian, no doubt searching for evidence that I'm lying. But, since I'm not, I stare back. I've got nothing to hide.

The intensity of his study eases, and he lets out a breath, sitting back in his chair again, apparently satisfied that I'm being truthful. 'Perhaps it's no surprise he didn't tell you,' he says. 'It doesn't exactly cast him in a favourable light.'

I don't know what to think of the sudden curiosity that pulls tight inside me, but I do know that I can't let it go. Antonio never gave any details on why he viewed Santiago with such bitterness, and I always thought it must have been about something dreadful, especially since his bitterness seemed to get worse as the years went on.

'What happened?' I ask.

'It's very simple,' Santiago says levelly. 'My father wasn't faithful to my mother. He had many affairs and I, unfortunately, found out about one of them after stumbling into a room at a family party, to find my father with one of his lovers.'

This doesn't surprise me. Antonio was very proud of his virility. It was why he hired me to be on his arm, and why he insisted we consummate our relationship— at least as much as he was physically able.

'That must have been awful,' I say and mean it, because it must have been. 'How old were you?'

'Twelve,' Santiago says. 'He swore me to secrecy, told me to never breathe a word of it to my mother. But I was furious with him for betraying her, and so I told her anyway.'

'He threw you out for that?' I ask, shocked.

Santiago's gaze is direct. 'Yes. Turned my mother and me out on the street. She found some peace in the bottom of a wine bottle and I found mine in physics.'

I want to believe he's lying to me, but I know a little of Santiago now and I know how he hates a lie. He wouldn't lie about this. What he's just said about Antonio's behaviour also rings true. He was a man who held grudges, and would fly into a rage over the slightest little thing. He was never awful to me—perhaps age had mellowed him—but I can see him doing exactly what Santiago said. Especially as a younger man.

'I'm so sorry,' I say, hearing how pathetic the words are but not knowing what else to say. 'That must have been terrible.'

'Why are you sorry?' The muscle in Santiago's jaw ticks again, anger flickering in his eyes, though I realise that this time it's not directed at me. 'It's not your fault. He never forgave me, did you know that? He shut me out. Left me and Mother without a penny. I tried to mend fences with him over the years, but he refused to answer any of my calls, or emails or texts.'

My chest tightens unexpectedly. Because beneath the fury in the words I can hear something else. Pain. 'You loved him,' I say without thinking. 'Didn't you?'

CHAPTER TWELVE

Santiago

THE OBSERVATION IS SHARP, a scalpel sliding into my flesh, and for a moment all I can do is sit there and stare at Beatrix. She's looking at me as if she knows me, as if all the emotions I cut from my heart years ago are still there. Even that most pathetic of all feelings: love.

Perhaps once, I loved him. Perhaps once, I thought him the greatest man who ever lived, and I wanted to be just like him. And perhaps once, he loved me in return. But I also told the truth once, and he held it against me forever.

Since then any love I once had for him curdled like sour milk, turning into a thin and bitter liquid that left a bad taste in my mouth. A taste easily got rid of with a couple of glasses of good Scotch.

But I don't want to talk about Antonio. She somehow led me into a conversation about him, asking questions that I had to give her the truth about. There's no sugar-coating her late husband's behaviour and I won't do it.

Of more pressing concern is her insistence on becoming my wife.

Marriage, like children, hasn't been on my radar, since it requires a level of emotional commitment that I'm not willing to give. It certainly only made my mother's life miserable. Then there's the fact that Beatrix is my father's widow, and I want nothing that was his.

Still, that conscience of mine kept whispering that what she was saying was correct, that she shouldn't be vilified for wanting some legal protection if she's to live with me here.

You didn't like the idea of her marrying someone else, either.

I shouldn't have said that about her never marrying another man, not so insistently. But the primitive man in me wouldn't be quiet. The thought of her choosing someone else *again* is not something I can bear, not before I've had my fill of her. She *has* to remain mine if she's going to be in my bed, there's no other option for me, and if a marriage vow will keep her at my side until we're done, then why not?

When we get tired of each other, we can separate, and what happens with our child we'll discuss then, since I'm not wedded to the idea of a family in the traditional sense. My mother and I were better off alone in the long run anyway.

'I don't want to talk about my father,' I say bluntly. 'The issue of a marriage is more pressing.'

Her eyes widen. 'Really? You seemed as if you didn't want to talk about that either.'

'I've changed my mind,' I say. 'The idea has some… merit.'

A flush of colour stains her cheekbones, and she takes another sip of her tea. 'If it would make you more comfortable with the idea, we could draw up some kind of contract. I mean, if you want a prenup, I'll sign it.'

A flicker of irritation goes through me. Does she think my discomfort with the idea of marriage is solely about money? That a prenup would make me feel 'comfortable'?

'This is not about my comfort,' I say, a little too sharply. 'A legal marriage will be for yours.'

She puts her cup down on the table, and leans back in her chair, regarding me. 'Why not yours? Is your comfort not important?'

It's an odd question, and one that sets me off balance, since I've never given much thought to my comfort or otherwise.

'I'm perfectly comfortable already,' I say curtly.

'Are you?' Her level gaze is strangely piercing. 'Is that why you're so angry all the time?'

Oh, she sees you. She sees you all too well.

My irritation turns into anger. I want to deny it, tell her she's wrong, but…

That would be a lie, wouldn't it? And aren't you always honest with yourself?

Anger simmers sullenly in my gut, proving the truth. I'm sitting here stiff as a board, because this woman has managed to get so completely under my skin that I can't get her out. She's been under it since the moment I saw her at that fundraiser, and it galls me that it's almost impossible for me to be my normal logical self when she's around.

But I'm a man who likes facts and those are the facts. I *can't* be my normal logical self when she's around. I have no physical self-control when she comes near, and all my efforts to deny that have failed. So now I'm forced to conclude that yes, I've been lying to myself about how much I want her, and that it's useless to pretend otherwise. Just as it's useless to pretend that everything she does doesn't either infuriate me or fascinate me, and usually both at the same time.

So once again, I give her the truth. 'What I'm angry about is having no self-control around you, because self-control is something I value.'

A look of surprise crosses her face, and this time I let myself have the feeling of satisfaction that I've surprised her. That I've made her feel as off-balance as I do.

Yet more colour floods through her cheeks, making her look like a blooming rose.

Her lashes lower abruptly, and she picks up her teacup again, taking a sip.

If it weren't for her blush and the way she's avoiding my gaze, I'd think my words have no effect on her at all. But I know better. She liked that I told her that, didn't she?

'That…goes both ways,' she murmurs into her teacup.

I like that. Her own need for me is something I already know, but hearing her admit it out loud is very satisfying.

'Is that why you chose my father?' I ask, surprising myself with the question and my own willingness to talk about it. Because now I'm giving it some rational thought, it's the only logical explanation. She's as uncomfortable as I am with our chemistry, and elected not to chase it.

Her lashes lift and her blue gaze meets mine, and I feel the impact like a blow to the stomach. It's like that first time in London, no anger, only fierce hunger, and this time my body tenses for a completely different reason entirely. For the first time she's letting me see this desire of hers, uncoloured by anything else, and it's as if she's giving me a gift.

'Yes,' she says. 'You affected me so powerfully and I was…afraid of it.'

I search her face, but there's only honesty there. 'Why?' I ask, curious now, though my hunger for her is rising again in equal measure, no matter that she knelt for me only an hour or so earlier.

'I…haven't felt that way about anyone before.' She's slightly hesitant, as if she can't find the right words, which for some reason is extremely erotic to me. 'It's… overwhelming.'

As I study her, my curiosity shifts and discovers a new and intense focus: her. Maybe I was…premature when I dismissed the idea of researching her as if she was a puzzle, deciding my desire was simple sexual attraction, nothing more. But there's merit to the thought of investigating her more thoroughly, and the scientist in me agrees. She's…interesting.

After that fundraiser, where I first saw her, I found out what I could about her. Then, after she rejected me, I let my anger at both her and my father colour my thinking. I let my anger at myself and my own lack of control around her get to me.

But this conversation, more honest and without anger, is letting me see her clearly for the first time. Letting me see her as I first did, at the bar, where she seemed to me the most beautiful woman I'd ever seen, and I wanted her.

I want her now, powerfully, yet I also want to discover the facts about her, get to know *her*.

I shift in my seat and lean forward. This is the first time she's shown me any vulnerability, confessed to feelings for me that aren't hate or simple lust, and I want to hear more. I want to know why she was so overwhelmed by me and why she'd never felt that way about anyone else before.

Still, maybe that can wait. For now, I'd like to hear about why she made the decision to choose my father instead of me. 'You didn't feel that even for my father?'

One corner of her mouth lifts in a faint smile, and my breath catches. I've seen her smile only once before, and that was when I approached her at the bar, and now I want it again. I want her mouth to curve in just that way, just for me. 'No, not at all for him,' she says. 'He was the…safer option.'

'Safer how?'

She's blushing again, as if my attention discomforts her yet pleases her, and I like that too. It's odd to imagine wanting to please her, since I've spent so long wanting to anger her, but her pleasure could be a research topic that I'd definitely consider immersing myself in.

'I…don't trust people easily,' she says, again sounding hesitant. 'My instincts can be wrong about them.'

My curiosity deepens still further. 'Why?' I ask. 'Did something happen to you?'

She glances away again, down at the cup in her hands. 'Oh, you don't want to know about all of that. It's really not very interesting.'

'*I'm* interested,' I tell her bluntly. 'You'll be my wife, in which case I'll want to know all the facts that relate to you.'

Again, her gaze lifts to mine and again I feel the impact of it. A punch of fascination and raw hunger. 'Okay,' she says. 'You asked for it. I was given into foster care as a baby and placed in a lot of different homes. It was very…destabilising. When I was around thirteen, another girl and I were actually placed with wonderful foster parents.' She pauses, shadows moving in her blue eyes. 'I thought they liked us, and when we were told they were considering adopting us, I was so excited. But at the last minute the other girl was adopted and I wasn't. I was never told why.'

There's a strange tightness in my chest. As if I empathise with her. I wasn't ever in foster care but I'm familiar with the sense of destabilisation. I felt that way myself, in my early childhood, with my parents and their acrimonious relationship that would at times spill over onto me. My father furious with me for something I said or did that he didn't agree with. My mother shaking me off and pulling away when she didn't want to deal with me.

The random element of it, the not understanding why they were so furious and dismissive, the not knowing what you had done that was wrong. It was all so precarious and fraught. Like living in a tent and being constantly afraid that a strong wind would come and blow it all down.

'I see,' I say. 'That must have been extremely confusing and difficult for you.'

She stares at me as if, again, I've said something surprising. Perhaps she wasn't expecting me to be sympathetic. 'You understand?' she asks, as if she's not really sure.

'Obviously, I didn't have the same experience as you,' I say. 'But I know what it's like to feel as if you're walking on shaky ground. For example, I don't know why Antonio could never forgive me for telling my mother about his affairs. He was angry, yes, but he stayed angry for so long, and I was only a child at the time. Also, my mother's mental health is not good, and that can be…challenging. I never know what's going to tip her over the edge, even now.'

'Oh, that sounds tough.' There's a crease between her brows, sympathy in her eyes. 'I'm sorry you had to deal with that.'

Again, she's completely genuine and the tightness in my chest gathers even tighter. It's not a feeling I enjoy. The things I had to do to look after my mother were necessary. Someone had to do them for her and, since I was her son, the task fell to me. It's not something that anyone has to apologise for.

'I managed,' I say, a little impatiently, since I'm not interested in talking about me. 'So, you have no family at all?'

'No,' she says and I catch a slight hint of a husk in her voice. This hurts her, doesn't it? 'Apparently my mother died having me, and my father gave me immediately into foster care, since he was too grief-stricken to care for me. I don't know who they were beyond that, and I don't want to.'

A sweeping anger grips me at this, but it's a different sort of anger this time. It's not directed at her, but for her. Grief I understand intellectually, but everything in me rebels at the thought of a father who gives away his baby because he can't deal with it. My own father did that, though his reasons were different and I was older, yet it only makes me even more sure that I will never do that to my own child.

In fact, looking into her blue eyes now, I see that same certainty reflected back. She won't either. On this, we agree totally.

Our gazes lock and hold, and something charges in the air between us, that familiar electric current. But this time there's a deeper element to it, as if the honesty of our conversation has added an understanding we didn't have before, and somehow this makes that current more intense.

Slowly, the blue in her eyes turns violet as the air around us constricts, sparking and crackling with heat.

'I'm not going to give you up,' I tell her abruptly, clearly. 'I want you in my bed and I want you now.'

CHAPTER THIRTEEN

Beatrix

THE SIMPLE STATEMENT hits me like an arrow, piercing me entirely.

I'm not going to give you up.

He means it too, because that's one thing I trust about Santiago. His honesty.

I wasn't expecting him to say that. I wasn't expecting to have this conversation at all. I was expecting more anger, more demands, more of him shoving his chair back and leaving, but, while he's certainly been angry, especially with that conversation about his father, he didn't leave.

Then he reconsidered my suggestion of us marrying, and that, too, I didn't expect. Or how I'd ended up confessing to him that my feelings for him were overwhelming before sharing with him facts about my own childhood.

I don't want to be vulnerable with him, though, which is why I chose anger, since it's stronger, safer. Yet I can't stay angry, not now. Not after catching a glimpse of the man behind the cold, furious scientist. The man formed from the child whose father didn't want him, just like mine didn't want me.

We have more common ground than I initially thought, which I hadn't anticipated. It's different, uncharted, and I don't like not knowing what will happen with him, with us, because I can't build a life on something as transient as physical hunger. At least with Antonio I knew from the first what kind of relationship it would be.

Then again, with the way Santiago is looking at me now and the things he's just said, physical hunger is a truth we share, and no matter how fleeting it might be, it's familiar. And given all the changes in my life so far, I need that familiarity. I crave it. It's not enough to build a life on, no, but it's a start.

You can't resist him anyway.

No, I can't.

I don't speak, but he shoves back his chair and rises to his feet. Then he holds out his hand to me in wordless invitation, his black gaze burning.

My decision is already made as I rise from my chair, too, and take his hand. His fingers wrap around mine, warm and strong, the leashed strength of his grip making every muscle in my body tighten with need.

We say nothing as he leads me inside and down the hallway to the graceful staircase. He's in no rush as he leads me up the stairs, slowly and with deliberation, and it winds my anticipation of what's to come tighter and tighter, making my heartbeat accelerate.

As we get to the top of the stairs, he leads me down

another hall, my mouth dry, my breathing short, and I let myself feel it. I let myself feel everything, the need, the craving. The desperation. The hunger.

It's dangerous to allow these feelings in, because they have the potential to make me far too vulnerable for comfort. But I'm tired of fighting them. Tired of pretending. Tired of feeling angry, too. I just want to surrender and let myself have this, have him, without any self-recriminations.

He pushes open a door at the end of the hallway, and pulls me inside, shutting it firmly behind us. Letting go of my hand, he moves over to the huge bed against one wall and flicks a switch, and soft, muted light spills into the room

If everything outside the room is historic, everything inside it is modern. Elements of the historic mansion are evident in the high ceilings and huge windows, but the room itself is carpeted with a deep, thick dark charcoal carpet that muffles all sound. The bed is a thick mattress set on a stepped platform, with a sleek dark wooden headboard behind and lots of shelving. Lush pillows, soft-looking sheets, and quilts make the bed plush and inviting.

It's a quiet, cosy room, with no distractions.

None except for him.

He comes back over to me, lifting his hands and cupping my face between them. His palms are warm against my skin, his dark eyes focused only on me. It's addicting when he looks at me this way. It's like the night we met, when we locked gazes and the rest of the world seemed to fall away.

That's part of why he's so dangerous, and why I chose his father over him, why I couldn't afford to get lost in any kind of affair with such an overwhelming man that I knew nothing about. But that seems a worry from a lifetime ago. Now all I want is that danger, that hunger, that pleasure. I want to be overwhelmed by him, by the way he looks at me, by the way he wants me.

No one else has ever wanted me the way he does, and I love it.

'You're the most passionate woman I have ever met,' he murmurs, obsidian eyes glittering with heat. 'Did you know that?'

My mouth is so dry I can barely speak, so all I do is shake my head.

'You should,' he goes on. 'You're beautiful, yes, but your passion is singular.'

I know I'm conventionally beautiful—after all, I've used it to survive. But no one has ever said that my passion was singular, as if it was an attribute instead of a flaw. No one has ever said anything about my passion at all.

I'm shivering with anticipation as I look up at him. 'You were always so furious with me,' I whisper, unable to stop myself from telling him this. 'I thought you hated me.'

He frowns, his thumbs stroking over my skin. 'I never hated you, Beatrix,' he says. 'Never. I told myself I did, but it seems as if I'm not as honest as I thought I was. Not with myself, at least. I was furious because

I wanted you. Because from the moment I saw you, I wanted you to be mine.'

There's a pressure in my chest, a lump in my throat. Part of me understands this already, since it was the only possible reason for his fury when I chose Antonio, not him. Yet I like that he admitted it, spoke the words out loud for me to hear.

'I can be yours,' I say. 'I can be yours for as long as you want me to be.' And in this moment I'm being completely honest with myself, and with him. And it feels good to say it. To give him what I know he still wants and what I want too.

The heat in his eyes glitters, black flames that threaten to burn me alive. Then he gives me the answer I'm dying for by lowering his head and covering my mouth with his, and I'm lost.

He's all heat, all demand, and as the kiss deepens it gets feverish, frantic. I'm leaning in to him, opening my mouth to him, letting him in to consume me, ravage me. My hands are on his chest, my fingers curling into the cotton of his shirt, trying to hold on to something to keep from being swept away.

But I should know better than that by now. There's no way to stop myself from drowning, nothing to cling to, and the only thing I can do is surrender to him, so that's what I do. I press myself against the hard length of his powerful body, pulling at his shirt, so I can get to the hot velvet of his skin. To touch him, put my mouth on him, feed the hunger inside me.

Except he's yanking down the zip of my dress and

pulling the fabric away even as I reach for his belt to unbuckle it.

'Stop,' he growls in warning. 'You've already had a taste. Now it's my fucking turn.' He tugs my hands away from him, releasing me only to turn me around so he can undo the zip of my dress all the way and pull the material down. I'm panting, every part of me burning, and I can barely stand still as he gets rid of my bra and knickers. Then I'm naked and suddenly I'm swept up in his arms as he carries me over to the platform bed, dumping me onto it on my back. Then he grips my hips, pulling me to the edge of the mattress as he goes down on his knees on the lowest step, and spreads my legs, holding them wide with his hands. He lowers his head and his mouth settles between my thighs, his tongue licking me like I'm an ice-cream cone melting on a hot summer day.

The pleasure is so sharp I cry out, arching up on the mattress. He grips me tighter, holding me in place as he licks and explores, nipping at my inner thighs, pushing his tongue inside me. He's feasting on me as if he hasn't had a decent meal in years, and I can't keep still. I writhe beneath the press of his wicked tongue, unable to keep the hoarse sounds he draws from me inside.

He's relentless, and before I can stop it the pleasure explodes without warning, drawing another harsh cry from my throat. His hands on me are firm as I shake and shake, but he doesn't move away. He keeps his mouth on me, continuing to work me with his tongue, until I'm shaking even harder, already building to another climax.

Then I cry out a third time, because he's stopping and I can't bear for him to. But he's only getting to his feet and ripping at his clothes, never taking his black gaze from mine.

I lie there trembling, amazed at myself and how much I want him mere minutes after the first orgasm. But as his clothes come off, all I can think of is how beautiful he is. Powerful shoulders and broad chest. Hard, muscled stomach. Lean waist. His skin a smooth, velvety olive.

He moves with a slow, athletic grace up the stairs to the bed, predatory and sleek as a panther as he stands there, looking down at me. I'm wrecked and ravaged by him, and there's no way to hide it, so I don't. I want him to see what he did to me and how much I still want him even after that.

'Yes, that's the way you should always be,' he murmurs, low and rough. 'Naked, with your legs spread, ready for me. Wanting me and only me.'

I love the way he says the words and the possessiveness note in them. They're erotic, making me feel claimed. No one has ever wanted me this way, to be theirs and only theirs. I've never been anyone's before and it's what I want. To be his. To be naked and ready for him, wanting him and only him.

He comes down over me, settling between my thighs, and I gasp as his body presses the length of mine. He's hot and heavy, and I'm pinned beneath him. Yet I don't feel trapped. I feel grounded, his weight another way he's claiming me for himself.

'Look at me,' he orders as he shifts, his hands sliding beneath my hips and lifting them slightly, angling me. 'Keep looking at me.'

And I do. I keep looking into his midnight eyes as I feel him push into me, so achingly slowly. It's as if he wants to feel every inch of me and is making me feel every inch of him, too. I shudder and gasp, even as I keep my gaze pinned to his, black velvet and glittering jet, and a hot, dark fire.

'Santiago,' I whisper helplessly as he slides deeper. 'Oh…my…*God*.'

He begins to move, and I know that the pleasure in his eyes he can also see in mine. I can't hide it from him, and I don't want to. I want him to see what he does to me, because it feels so good. So good, I can't bear it. So good, I want more of it.

His control is perfect, and he moves with the same rhythm, slow, relentless, and I'm coming again, my hands gripping his shoulders, my nails digging into his skin, crying out his name.

He doesn't stop. He keeps going at that same slow, deliberate pace until I'm twisting beneath him, begging him to keep going, and not to stop, don't ever stop.

It was never like this with Antonio, the only other man I've been with. He didn't care about my pleasure, only his own, but Santiago has apparently made my pleasure his entire focus, using my movements and my cries to either speed up or slow down. Drawing it out until I'm sobbing for release.

Only when the third orgasm approaches does he let himself go, upping the pace and driving harder and faster, until he slides a hand between us, adding to the friction by stroking my clit until, as relentless as a crashing wave, the pleasure inside me breaks and crushes me beneath it.

Only then does he take what he wants for himself, his arms tightening around me as he growls out his release in my ear.

CHAPTER FOURTEEN

Santiago

BEATRIX AND I stand together before a low table in the room designated for marriage ceremonies. It's been a couple of days since we arrived back from Spain, and now we're in the town hall, where all legal marriages happen in France, waiting for the ceremony to begin.

I have expedited all the paperwork, so everything is in order, and one of the mayor's delegates is standing behind the table, ready to perform the ceremony. I've been assured it won't take long, which is just as well, since I want to be able to claim my new wife in a different, more personal way, and as quickly as possible.

Beatrix is standing beside me, her hands clasped tightly together. I told her not to bother to dress for the occasion if she didn't wish to, but apparently Helene decided that Beatrix needed to mark it in some way, and found her a dress of white silk to wear. It's form-fitting around the bodice, cupping her beautiful breasts, with frothy skirts that fall to her knees. Her long golden hair is loose and she holds a single white rose in one hand.

She looks stunningly, impossibly beautiful.

It's a very different wedding from the one she had with my father, who turned it into a big, splashy affair in the cathedral in Toledo, with hundreds of guests. Then she wore an ornate gown with long skirts and a train, a silken veil, and a diamond tiara. And I know this because I looked at each and every press photograph there was, blindly furious. I told myself I had to know as much as possible about the wedding so I could answer any questions my mother had about it, so she didn't have to look at the pictures herself. But of course that wasn't the only reason. I wanted to see if Beatrix was smiling. I wanted to know if she was enjoying her wedding day, if she was happy to be marrying the man she'd chosen over me.

I never found out the answer to that question, yet now I'm the one standing next to her, and there is no cathedral, no crowds, no wedding dress costing hundreds of thousands of euros, no press.

There is only us, the mayor's delegate, who will preside over the ceremony, and a couple of witnesses brought in for the occasion.

We didn't discuss what kind of wedding we wanted, because there was no reason to. This is happening because she required it, and I agreed. It's purely legal and not symbolic in any way.

Not that we've had a moment to discuss anything. Not when I've taken full advantage of her promise to be in my bed, and have been keeping her there every opportunity I get.

That first night we had, where she was fully mine at last, was incendiary. I couldn't get enough of her taste, her cries, her hands in my hair, and her nails in my skin. I couldn't get enough of how she came apart in my arms so beautifully, each and every time, and I made a vow there and then that I would ruin her for any other man.

Since then I've approached that goal with a single-mindedness that equals my single-mindedness in the lab when testing a new design. Trying different pressures, different scenarios, checking every component to make sure they're all performing at the optimal level.

She never protests, reaching for me as hungrily as I reach for her, taking everything I give her, then giving back in return. Her passion is electric. I'm obsessed, and our mutual hunger shows no sign of waning any time soon.

That doesn't concern me, though. She'll be my legal wife in a few minutes, and then we'll spend the night together, consummating this marriage in every way possible. Perhaps it'll take weeks for this need to disappear, perhaps a month. Perhaps it won't go away until after the baby is born. It doesn't matter, since it *will* go away eventually—physical passion always does—and then we'll have to decide how best to separate.

In the meantime, there's lots of pleasure to be had, and I aim to gorge myself on every drop of it.

The ceremony proceeds and within ten minutes

we're signing the documents on the table. I sign first then stand back to let Beatrix have her turn. Her hand doesn't shake as she signs her name, a name that will not change even though I have married her.

This irritates me. I wanted everything to be different from her first marriage, yet the fact that she gets to keep his name, that she had it from him first, needles me. That I'm even irritated at all needles me. I should have got past this by now. He's dead, beyond my reach and hers, and besides, she didn't marry him because she loved him.

She didn't marry you because she loves you.

No, but love was never going to be part of any marriage we had anyway. Still, I can't shake the feeling of annoyance. I didn't bother with rings, since again, this union is purely legal, but now I'm regretting the decision. At least choosing a ring for her would make it different, because it would be *my* ring she'd be wearing.

I find myself watching her as she signs the documents, looking for a smile, for a sign that this is something that makes her happy, though why I should want her to be happy is beyond me. Perhaps it's because those smiles in her previous wedding photos were all fake, and I want something genuine from her. Something that's mine and only mine.

Her passion is yours and only yours.

Yes, that's true. Perhaps I'll have to be satisfied with that.

She straightens and stands aside for the witnesses, one man and one woman, who are waiting to sign the documents too. As the woman finishes signing, Beatrix smiles and holds the rose out to her.

It's real, that smile. It's genuine, and it makes something tight and painful gather behind my breastbone. It feels almost like jealousy, that this stranger should earn a beautiful smile and a flower as a gift from her. From *my* wife.

Her smiles are few, and I have earned a couple in bed, but only there. They should be mine, her smiles, all of them should be mine like that very first one was mine, and for this woman to earn one by simply signing a piece of paper infuriates me.

Why should you care who she smiles at?

I shouldn't care and I know this. She's mine now, I have the documents to prove it, and yet it feels…as if that's not enough. Even her passion being mine is not enough, no matter how I tell myself I'll have to be satisfied with it, and I don't know why I feel this possessive when she was the one who suggested we marry in the first place.

I need to crush this jealousy and possessiveness. It's purely a biological response and I need to ignore it. I already have her in the one place I wanted her, and that's in my bed.

The woman takes the rose Beatrix offers her, and smiles back, giving her a pretty *merci*, while I stand here like a fool, being jealous of a stranger.

'You look like a thundercloud,' Beatrix observes as we make our exit from the room. 'What's wrong? Too late to change your mind about marrying me now.'

Her tone is light, the remains of her smile playing

around her pretty mouth. She's so stunningly lovely. She's *my* wife now, I have to remember that, and getting angry because I want more of her smiles is an irrational response. Still, I can't help the urge to make this wedding different from her first, and so I've decided on something.

'Nothing is wrong,' I say, taking her hand as we walk down the town hall's steps to where my driver waits with the car. 'I've decided to make a quick stop on the way home, however.'

'Oh?' She glances at me as we get into the car. 'Why?'

'Because we're missing something,' I say.

She gives me a curious look. 'Missing what?'

I'm very tempted not to tell her, to make it a surprise, but I can't think of any logical reason to do that. So I say, 'A ring.' Then as my driver gets into the front seat, I instruct him to take us to one of Paris's most exclusive and expensive jewellery showrooms.

Beatrix is frowning at me, no sign of her smile this time as the car pulls away from the kerb. 'I don't need a ring, Santiago.'

'I disagree,' I say coolly. 'It's a good reminder that you're my wife.'

'A reminder? I'm hardly likely to forget.'

Annoyed at myself for my ill-chosen words, I once again have to force myself to relax and not to snap. 'A wedding present, then,' I say, trying to match her earlier lightness. 'And an apology for my appalling behaviour towards you.'

Her frown doesn't lift though. 'You don't need to

get me a wedding present and you've already apologised—'

'Let me do this, Beatrix,' I interrupt before my temper can cause any more issues. 'Please. I would like to.'

She stares at me for a moment, and then her frown eases, her mouth softening. I'm not sure what she saw in my face, but there's something in her eyes I don't recognise and it makes my chest feel a little hollow. 'Okay,' she says simply. 'That would be lovely.'

I'm disconcerted by her easy capitulation, especially when I'm used to fighting with her, and something in my face must have given me away, because she gives a soft laugh. 'I'm not plotting your death, Santiago. I promise.'

'Why would I think that?' I ask, even more disconcerted that she managed to read me with such ease.

Her eyes are alight, sparkling like tiny blue stars. 'Because you gave me an incredibly suspicious look.'

I want to tell her she's wrong, but she's not, so I give her the truth. 'I was expecting some kind of protest, I have to admit,' I say. 'I'm not used to you just giving in.'

Her lashes lower, blue gleaming from beneath them. 'Really? After the past few nights?'

A flash of heat grips me by the throat, and I want to pull her into my arms, sit her in my lap, lift her white skirts and sink myself into the luscious heat between her thighs. Make her give in to me here as she does in bed every night.

But I've decided on the ring now, and I will have it on her finger, and besides, there's plenty of time for pleasure later. So all I do is lock gazes with her, letting her see the intention in my eyes, and I can't resist the triumph that fills me when she blushes like a summer sunrise.

That's genuine, that response. There's nothing fake about her desire for me or about the pleasure she takes from my touch. Her orgasms are real, too, and that's more than she ever got from my father.

The jeweller's showroom is by appointment only, but they instantly make time for me when I give them my name. We're shown into an elegant salon with white velvet couches and a white carpet. Glass cases show off the jewellery to perfect effect.

Beatrix's eyes are wide as the sales assistant leads us to one of the couches and we sit down. I instruct the man to bring us a selection of wedding rings, including ones that have an engagement ring to match, since that's important too.

'Please don't buy me anything too expensive,' Beatrix murmurs as the man vanishes through a door.

I'm sitting next to her and, after that flirtatious look in the car just before, the warmth of her thigh pressing against mine is making it difficult to think properly. 'Why not?' I ask, curious as to why she's uncomfortable, since I can see that she is. 'You're the wife of a very rich man. Shouldn't you have something expensive?'

Her hands are clasped in her lap, her attention roving around the room. 'Our marriage is for legal purposes only and for the baby. Rings…mean something.'

'So why did you wear that diamond my father

bought for you?' I ask, unable to help myself. 'Did that mean something?'

A spark of anger glitters in her eyes and she sits a little straighter. 'This is about Antonio? You know why I married him, Santiago. I told you.'

I want to tell her that no, it's got nothing to do with him, but again, that would be a lie. 'Well, you're marrying me for the same reasons.'

'Yes,' she says, the word sharp. 'I am. To protect myself and the baby. If that's a problem for you, then you should have said.'

Why do you hurt people all the time? That's all you ever do. You just can't help yourself.

The thought is barbed and painful, so I push it away, even as I struggle to keep hold of a temper that shouldn't be as out of control as it is. 'It's not a problem for me,' I say, attempting to moderate my tone.

She gives me a disbelieving look, then drops her gaze to her hands. 'You need to stop throwing him back in my face,' she says. 'I married him because I had nothing. I didn't finish high school and I had no qualifications. I couldn't get a decent-paying job. I was barely scraping by, and I wanted a life. I wanted options. I wanted a home and a family, and that's what I thought marrying Antonio would get me.' She glances at me, blue eyes burning. 'Do you know what it's like to have nothing and no one? To have no family and no prospects, and no future except more of the same? It's lonely, Santiago. And bleak.'

I study her, and for a moment I can see everything in her eyes, all her painful vulnerabilities. Loneliness, despair, fear. And I remember what she told me the night she arrived, about how she was given up by her father into foster care, and how the one family she wanted to stay with didn't want her in the end.

All of a sudden, I'm disgusted with myself. Disgusted by my jealousy and how I can't let it go that she married my father, not me. Disgusted by my anger at her, which has been and is completely unwarranted.

Holding on to anger is what your father did too, remember?

Oh, I remember. Just as I remember telling myself I'd be different.

So I reach out and take her hand, sliding my fingers through hers and gripping tight. Meet her gaze, so painfully blue. 'I'm sorry that happened to you,' I say, meaning every word. 'And, while I don't know what it's like to have no family, I do know what it's like to have no prospects.'

'You?' Her fingers tighten in mine, as if she likes me holding her hand. As if she needs it. 'I find that difficult to believe.'

I like the way she's gripping me, looking at me as if she's interested, as if she's curious. So I say, 'My mother worked herself to exhaustion to keep a roof over our heads after my father threw us out. So I decided that when I grew up I was going to take care of her, since he wouldn't.'

'What did you do?'

'I had a gift for science,' I say. 'Physics in particular. I worked extremely hard at school, got into university early, and then got my PhD. I have a gift for numbers too, so at the same time I played with the stock market and accumulated enough for a research start-up. Then I went looking for investors in the tech sector.'

'What happened then?' Her anger has gone now, leaving behind it an open curiosity that I like more and more, since most people aren't that curious about me as a person. They want my ideas and my expertise, my talent, and now my money. Even the lovers I have aren't interested in who I am. Then again, I've never wanted them to be, so it's strange to now be enjoying Beatrix's interest.

'I had a couple of wealthy investors interested, and the company grew from there.' I slide my thumb over her soft skin in an absent caress, relishing the feel of her skin against mine.

She nods. 'I don't have the same rags-to-riches story that you do, but… Well, I worked in a supermarket stacking shelves, and a co-worker told me she was going to apply to be on this sugar-baby website in order to get more cash. And I thought *Why not?* I didn't have the education or gifts that you do, but… I'm not unattractive, so I used that.'

I look at her lovely face, hear the catch in her voice as she speaks, and I realise that in many ways we're alike. Both of us using what we had in order to survive. But there's more to her than merely a pretty face. She must have had a lot of strength and determination to get through what seems to have been an appalling upbringing. Certainly, she's been nothing but strong and determined with me.

She's a woman capable of achieving anything she sets her mind to. You'd employ her in a heartbeat.

Yes. I would.

'Antonio was well aware I needed money,' she goes on. 'I didn't take advantage of him, and he didn't take advantage of me. We had an agreement that satisfied us both.' She pauses a moment, then says, 'He told me he didn't want you to inherit, and that's why he married me. Did he…tell you that?'

Oh, I know. He flung that in my face the last time I visited him in a last-ditch effort to put our differences aside.

'Remember that day I turned up at the estate?' I ask, continuing to caress the back of her hand with my thumb. 'Not long after your wedding?'

Her cheeks flush and her eyes darken. 'I remember.'

Yes, I remember, too. How Antonio and I shouted at each other out the front of the hacienda and how, as I turned away to leave, I'd caught a glimpse of Beatrix at the window, staring at me.

'That's what he told me,' I say. 'That he married you to make sure I didn't get the estate. So you were right, that's exactly why.'

Her fingers tighten around mine as if I'm the one needing comfort, and her blue gaze is very direct. 'He was wrong to do that,' she says quietly. 'I thought it was wrong then and it's still wrong now.'

CHAPTER FIFTEEN

Beatrix

It's strange to sit here in this luxurious jewellery showroom, holding my new husband's hand, having a discussion about my previous marriage to his father.

It's also strange that we're having a somewhat normal conversation, when our interactions have either been furious or, certainly for the past couple of days, entirely physical.

It's strange to be married, too. To have another husband so soon after my first, and that my new husband is the man I thought I hated above all others.

Except I don't hate him, I know that, and perhaps I never did. It's only that he's complicated and so are my feelings about him. He's so controlled out of the bedroom, so ruthlessly self-possessed. The only time he ever seems free is when he's in bed with me, where all the passion inside him comes roaring out like a forest fire. He's a man of extremes who can't find a middle ground—he's either burning hot or icy cold, with no in-between. It's unexpectedly fascinating.

He is unexpectedly fascinating.

The wedding ceremony we just had, though, was almost the antithesis of my first wedding. That was in the cathedral in Toledo, with all of Antonio's friends and acquaintances, the cream of the Spanish aristocracy. My wedding dress then was studded with crystals, ornate and heavy, with a huge train, a veil and a tiara. It was a surreal experience to go from stacking supermarket shelves to marrying a much older man in a cathedral, wearing a dress that cost over a hundred thousand euros. And then to attend a wedding party in an exclusive hotel that cost even more… None of it was my decision. Antonio wanted to have a big, splashy wedding to show me off, to display his much younger trophy wife to as many people as possible, and, despite feeling like a fraud the whole time, I went along with it. He wanted to marry me and make me a duchess, so protesting just seemed ungrateful.

This time, however, the only dress I had was one Helene somehow procured for me. I told her what I wore didn't matter, but she insisted. It didn't matter that I'd been married before, she said, a woman should always wear something pretty on her wedding day. And the dress *was* pretty. So I put it on, and she gave me a rose to carry, and in the end I was glad I'd worn the dress. It was simple, nothing splashy about it, which made it much more my style, and also because Santiago's eyes flared the moment he saw me.

There was nothing romantic about the ceremony, yet I had a strange, fluttery, excited feeling in my stomach all the same. And afterwards, as I handed one of the witnesses my rose, I caught a glimpse of Santiago's face and the strange fury burning in his eyes. It disappeared the instant I asked him what was wrong, though, so I'm not sure what had annoyed him so intensely.

I made a mental note to ask him when we got back home, because I didn't want him to be angry. I didn't want to return to us being furious with each other, not when these past few days have been so good. It's been only physical, admittedly, but I love being in his bed. I love the pleasure he gives me, and afterwards I love how he holds me. No one has ever just held me.

But then he mentioned buying a ring, and, while I didn't think we needed one, it seemed important to him, so I agreed. This jewellery showroom is far too luxurious and expensive, though, and I didn't want him spending so much money on rings that mean nothing. But then he mentioned Antonio yet again, and I got tired of it. I had to give him the context for my decision to marry his father, tell him where I came from, and what I was trying to leave behind, and I wanted him to understand, because constantly fighting about it is tiring.

He surprised me, however, by actually listening to me. Then he gave me a little piece of his own history in return. I hadn't expected that from him. Which is now why I want to let him know that his father was wrong. Antonio was wrong about a lot of things, but most specifically he was wrong to disinherit his son, wrong to stay so angry with him, and for so long, too.

Santiago's fingers in mine are warm, and the look

in his dark eyes burns. So I go on, 'It wasn't fair of him and it wasn't right. I did actually try to talk to him about it, but he wouldn't listen to me.'

'You tried to talk to him about me?' His attention is so focused on me it's as if nothing else in the world exists for him, as if what I'm saying is of such vital importance that he can't look away even for a moment. It's intoxicating.

'Yes,' I say and it's true. I did try to talk to Antonio about Santiago, and more than a few times. But he refused to even engage. 'I'd like to think there was a part of him that wanted to make things right with you, but he let his anger get in the way.'

Santiago begins to say something, then the sales assistant returns with several black velvet trays, interrupting the moment.

Santiago releases my hand, the warmth of his skin lingering. I'd much rather be holding it, and continuing our conversation, than looking at these rings, but the sales assistant is now pointing out each piece and the opportunity for more conversation slips away.

I have no choice but to study the rings in the trays, and to listen to the assistant's patter. Antonio bought me a massive diamond as an engagement ring, but I only wore it a couple of times. It was too showy, too flashy for my taste, and the rings in these trays, while beautiful, are all showy and flashy, too. They're rings someone buys either for love or to prove a point, and I want to ask Santiago what kind of point he's trying to prove, since it's definitely not about love.

Reaching for one at random, I put it on my finger,

only for Santiago to shake his head and offer another choice, this one with a huge sapphire. They're all eye-wateringly expensive, even the simpler ones, and I'm getting more and more uncomfortable. He's not buying a ring for me. He's buying a ring for himself, and I want to know why.

Eventually, I take off the fifth choice, a giant ruby, and put it back in the tray, then glance at him. 'I appreciate the thought, Santiago,' I say levelly, 'but exactly what point are you trying to make here? I already have one enormous ring I don't wear, so why would I need another?'

His dark gaze flashes, always a sure sign of his temper, and I brace myself for whatever furious retort is going to come out of his mouth. But then he lets out a breath, abruptly waves away the assistant, then turns on the couch to face me. 'I want to tell you that I'm not trying to make a point,' he says in a quieter voice than I'm expecting, 'but I suppose you're right. I am.'

'It's not about buying me a wedding present at all, is it?'

'No.' His gaze is direct, hiding nothing. 'I want your marriage to me to be different from the marriage you had with my father.'

I frown. 'Please don't tell me you're *still* jealous of him.'

'I didn't think I was,' he says honestly. 'But apparently I am. And apparently it's not only him I'm jealous of. I was jealous of the woman you gave your rose to, because you smiled at her and you hardly ever smile at me.'

The words are little shocks, each pulsing through me, jolting me. I know he was jealous of Antonio, that's always been obvious, but I thought it was more about his estrangement from his father than it was about me.

It's wrong to feel good about his jealousy, because jealousy can be ugly. Yet I feel good about it all the same. Because it's not only my body he wants, he wants my smiles, too, and I can't think why they're important to him, but they are.

'I want a ring on your finger,' he goes on bluntly. 'I want *my* ring on your finger.'

The possessiveness in his voice makes me feel even better, since no one has ever said that to me before. Not that they wanted *me*. And it makes me feel possessive in return. 'What about a ring for you?' I ask. 'I promised you I'd be faithful, but you didn't promise me the same thing.'

His gaze flickers, black sparks glittering there. 'Do you want me to be faithful to you? I didn't think you'd care.'

'I didn't think I would either,' I say truthfully. 'But I do care. I don't want you sleeping with other women. Only me.'

His beautiful mouth curls in a shockingly sexy smile that makes every inch of my skin tighten in response. 'Does the thought of me sleeping with other women make you jealous, wife of mine?'

Wife of mine...

I shiver at the words and at his smile, because I *am* his wife. For some reason I feel more his wife than I ever was Antonio's. 'Yes,' I say, giving him another truth to keep. 'It does.'

His smile now is full of male satisfaction, but I don't mind that. I like it, even. 'Good,' he says. 'Hold that thought.'

Without a word, he rises to his feet and goes over to the counter and the sales assistant, and says a few words to him. A few moments later Santiago returns, sits down next to me again, and opens one hand.

Sitting in the centre of his palm are two rings of white gold. Simple, elegant bands and unadorned, one bigger and one smaller. He picks up the smaller of the two and says, 'Give me your hand.'

As I do, my stomach flutters with nervous anticipation, which gets worse as he pushes the simple band onto my ring finger. It feels heavy there, like his arms around me, holding me. I swallow as he gives me the larger ring before holding out his own hand. 'Your turn,' he says, his dark eyes alight with challenge. 'Claim your husband, pretty Bea.'

My name is never shortened. I'm always Beatrix to everyone because no one knows me well enough to shorten it. I've never *let* anyone know me well enough. Even Antonio only ever called me Beatrix. Perhaps I should be offended by Santiago calling me Bea, since it's assuming a level of relationship that we don't have. Yet I'm not offended. It's the opposite, a flush warming my cheeks, a warm glow sitting in my chest.

Dangerous.

It is dangerous. This feeling inside me, this glow, this warmth. It's the needy part of me that wants affection, tenderness, connection. It's the part of me that's the most vulnerable and the easiest to hurt. It loves that he shortened my name, because it implies affection, and it loves him promising me he'd be faithful, then challenging me to claim him, as if he wants me to choose him. As if he wants to be mine.

And you want to be his. You always did.

Maybe I did the night I first saw him. But it was only the briefest of fantasies. Because being his involves opening myself up to him and trusting him, and he's given no evidence that trust is important to him or even something he wants. Which means no matter how he looks at me with challenge and heat, and calls me Bea, I can't let him in. I can't give him that trust, it's too dangerous, especially with that needy part of me wanting so much more than he would ever want to give.

I drop my gaze to his hand as I slide the ring on his finger without a word. But of course he picks up on my hesitation.

'What's wrong?' he asks. 'You don't like the rings? I chose the plainest and simplest of the bands.'

I could lie, pretend nothing's wrong, but I need to know where I stand. I need to know what this marriage will be, because we haven't discussed it, and we need to.

I release his hand and look up at him. 'It's not the rings,' I say.

He tilts his head, studying me, eyes narrowing. 'Then what? You're regretting marrying me already?'

'No,' I say, 'but I need to know what kind of marriage we're going to have.'

Impatience flickers across his face. 'Haven't we had this discussion?'

'We didn't talk about specifics,' I say. 'I know we promised to be faithful to each other, but am I going to live with you? Will we be sleeping together regularly? What about our assets? Do we—'

'It will be a marriage,' he interrupts, his tone slightly edged. 'A marriage in every way, except for the fact that we're not in love.'

There's no reason I should feel a sharp pain as he says that, but I do. Which is ridiculous, because he's right. We're not in love, of course we're not in love, and I don't want to be, especially not with him.

Shoving the pain aside, I ask, 'But what does that mean? What does it look like? Antonio and I had separate rooms, and we had separate lives, too. Are you thinking along those lines? And what happens when we don't want to sleep together any more? Will you expect me to move out?'

His impatience has turned into annoyance now, and it glitters hotly in his dark eyes. 'Do you really need to know all of that now?'

He doesn't want to talk about this, even I can see that, but I'm loath to let it go. 'Why?' I ask. 'You have something better to do?'

This time it's not annoyance that's glowing hot in his eyes, but something else. Something familiar. 'Of course I have something better to do,' he says in a low voice. 'I want to take my new wife to bed.'

It's impossible to resist the desire in his gaze. It makes the throb between my thighs insistent, makes me forget what I'm saying, even forget how to breathe. Perhaps I shouldn't keep pushing this. Perhaps I should leave it, since it is, after all, our wedding day, and I'm more than ready for the pleasure I know only he can give me. And apart from anything else, I'm tired of fighting.

So I let go of my questions and this time purposefully give him a smile, one that he doesn't need to be jealous about. One that's just for him. 'Well,' I murmur, 'when you put it like that, how can I refuse?'

CHAPTER SIXTEEN

Santiago

I OPEN MY eyes and stare at the ceiling for a couple of moments, my brain, for a change, blissfully empty of thought. I'm relaxed, sated, and feel better than I have for months, if not years. A warm hand is resting on my stomach, golden hair lying across my chest, so I turn my head and there she is, fast asleep beside me.

My wife.

Things had the potential to be difficult when I bought her the ring yesterday, which Beatrix was clearly unhappy about. But then she gave me her reasons for it and I won't lie, I felt a measure of satisfaction that she didn't wear my father's engagement ring. But I had to tell her the truth about why I wanted her to wear mine, that I was jealous of the smiles she gave so freely to everyone but me. She liked my jealousy, though—that blush of hers gave her away, and certainly enough to get a promise from me to be faithful to her. Not that it's a problem in any case. No woman I've ever been with—and I've been with many—has ever given me the kind of pleasure she does, so it was nothing to tell her I wanted only her. It's the truth, after all.

I prop myself up on my elbow, studying her sleeping face. The perfection of her mouth. The straight line of her nose. The arched golden brows. The pale, silky skin. Her other hand is tucked beneath her chin, and I can see the gleam of my wedding band around her finger.

Deep satisfaction stretches out inside me, the primitive man pleased at this display of my claim on her. The unadorned white gold rings were a good choice, I could see that as soon as I showed them to her, and that she liked them pleases me. Last night I staked my claim on her in other ways, leaving my marks on her pale skin, and now I ease the sheet down to her waist in order to admire them.

I had no idea that possessing her would make me feel this way, so self-satisfied and smug, and not a little triumphant, and, since she's mine unequivocally, I allow myself to enjoy the feelings for a few moments.

So, now she's yours, what's next?

An interesting question. Obviously what's next is the baby and we need to discuss our plans for its arrival. I have a room next to this one that is at present a guest room, but I'll have it converted into the perfect nursery.

What about those things she asked of you yesterday?

Through the haze of satisfaction, something unwelcome shifts inside me, a nagging irritation.

It's true I was annoyed when she asked for the details of our marriage going forward. Mainly because all

I could think about was the best way to get her home and into bed as quickly as possible. I didn't want to discuss the minutiae of what our lives would look like now we're married, not then at least.

Now, though, I'm reflecting on the conversation, and I can see why those details would be important to her. She wants stability and certainty, and I understand that, especially since in her early life she had neither. She wants a home, too, and a family, and again, I understand.

Bringing her here to Paris has been very much about what *I* want, even if the marriage itself was her suggestion, and now she's my wife, she's my responsibility. Which means it's my duty to take care of her, provide her with what she needs, what she wants, and that, at least, I'm familiar with. I've been providing for my own mother since I left school, after all, even if she gives me no thanks for it.

Beatrix makes a soft sound, giving a sensual little stretch in her sleep as she rolls onto her back, and the sheet falls away, exposing her full breasts and the marks of my mouth on her skin. My gaze roves further down her body, to the soft curve of her stomach where our baby lies.

Hunger begins to build inside me, and I'm getting hard again. I'd have thought that after the night we had together, and all the pleasure it involved, I wouldn't be so hungry again or so soon, but I am.

I want to touch her, wake her with kisses before sinking inside her tight, wet heat, but I kept her up till the early hours of the morning, and she needs sleep.

So instead I slip from the bed, pull on a pair of jeans, and leave the room.

Downstairs, I go into the kitchen, where Helene is bustling about, and arrange for a breakfast tray to be brought up to us. While she's doing that, she says absently, 'Oh, by the way, your mother phoned last night. I told her you weren't to be disturbed.'

Fuck. Of course. My mother's nightly call. I'd forgotten entirely about it, and I know my mother: she doesn't like to be forgotten.

I'll have to call her back, since if I don't she gets upset, so, moving quietly, I retrieve my phone from the bedroom, then go back downstairs and outside to the terrace to make the call.

'Where were you last night, Santiago?' my mother demands immediately on answering. 'You didn't tell me you were out.'

'It slipped my mind,' I say levelly. 'Hence me calling you now.'

'Oh, I see,' she says, sounding hurt. 'I'm that easy to forget, am I?'

It's always this way with Catelina. She wants attention, and gets wounded if she feels she's not being given an adequate amount of it. I'm eternally having to reassure her, which can be a long and involved task that requires patience. 'It wasn't like that,' I point out mildly. 'I had an...unexpected engagement.'

'What engagement?'

And abruptly I'm confronted with my own insistence on the truth, and how, years ago, I made a promise to myself that I would never lie to her, not after my father lied to her so completely. Yet once again I find myself in the position of having to give her a truth that will hurt, about Beatrix and me, and there's no way around it. No way to soften it.

Then again, as she keeps telling me so eloquently, nothing I do ever makes her feel better, so I may as well just say it. She'll find out at some point anyway.

'There's something I should tell you,' I say, keeping my tone neutral. 'I know you were hoping that I'd find a wife. And, well, I did.'

A shocked silence echoes down the other end of the phone.

'That's what I was doing yesterday,' I go on. 'I was getting married.'

'Oh, Santiago,' she says at last, her voice wavering. 'I can't tell you how happy this makes me.'

My heart feels painful, because of course this will *not* make her happy. Nothing I do for her ever does, and she never lets me forget it.

'Don't speak too soon,' I say. 'You don't know who I married.'

'Well, of course I don't,' she says irritably. 'Especially since the last time we spoke, you gave no hint that you were even considering getting married.'

My patience frays, not so much at her, but at myself for drawing this out. The truth will upset her, but the sooner she knows, the sooner she can come to terms with it.

'It's Beatrix, Mother,' I say. 'And she's expecting my child.'

Silence echoes down the phone, and I stare straight

ahead, at the oak tree in front of me, the sound of the fountain filling the dead quiet.

'Beatrix,' my mother repeats, as if the name means nothing to her.

'Father's widow.'

Again there's a silence and I can hear her breathing.

'Her?' she asks, shocked now. 'You married *her*?'

'She's pregnant,' I say, my tone flat. 'We thought it best for the baby if we got married.'

My mother breathes faster now, working herself up into a state. 'I can't believe it,' she whispers. 'I can't believe you married *her*. You must know what that would do to me, Santiago! You must know!'

Every muscle in my body tenses, the sound of her hurt like a knife in my chest.

All you ever do is hurt her. You can't help it.

I ignore the whisper in my head, harden my heart to the pain. I can do nothing for her now, just as I could do nothing for her then, only give her a truth she doesn't want to hear. A reality that must be faced whether she likes it or not.

'Yes, I do know.' There's nothing else I can say and sugarcoating it won't help. It never does. 'I'm sorry.'

'No, you're not!' The sound of her betrayal echoes down the phone. 'Why would you marry that…that… *slut*? Of all the women you've been with, why *her*?'

She's getting angry, and she has a right to be. But I won't have her calling Beatrix names. 'Don't call her that,' I say warningly. 'She's my wife now and she's carrying your grandchild, and I'm sorry, Mother. I really am. But that's the reality.'

I wait for a response, but there isn't one, because she's ended the call.

Anger coils and knots in my gut, and it takes every ounce of will I have not to hurl the phone to the ground and watch it break into tiny pieces. But I won't, because that won't help anything, just as calling her back won't help anything. She can't see anything but her own pain, even though that initial betrayal was over twenty years ago now. She's blinded by it, wedded to her hurt the way my father was wedded to his anger, and nothing will change her mind. Especially not me.

A warm hand suddenly settles in the middle of my back, and I turn around to find Beatrix standing there. Her golden hair is loose, and she's wearing the white shirt I wore to our wedding, and nothing else. Her blue eyes are luminous as they stare up into mine, though there's a slight crease between her brows.

'What was all that about?' she asks, searching my face. 'Are you okay?'

For a moment I can't speak. She's looking at me as if she's worried about me, and her first question is about whether I'm okay, and I can't remember the last time someone asked me that. I can't remember the last time anyone cared about my wellbeing enough to even ask…certainly neither of my parents ever did.

'Santiago?' she asks softly when I don't reply, the crease between her brows deepening.

I should pretend nothing's wrong, that I'm not furious, that I'm okay. But again, the truth is important and I'm not a hypocrite.

It'll probably hurt her, though.

Fuck. I don't want to tell her what my mother thinks of her, or what she said about her. It seems that no matter what I do, the truth ends up hurting someone.

I reach for her, my palms settling on her hips as I pull her close, fitting her warm, silky body against mine. 'What did you hear?' I ask.

Colour flushes her cheeks. 'I heard a little. I know, I shouldn't have been listening. I just woke up and you weren't there, so I came to find you. I heard your voice and followed it.' She puts her hands on my bare chest, her palms warm, and for a change her touch eases my tension, sanding away the sharp edges of my anger.

It's strange to be touched for comfort's sake instead of for pleasure, yet it's not unwelcome. It feels…good.

'You don't want to know,' I murmur, sliding my hands over the rounded curves of her bare behind. I want her closer, I want as much of her warmth as I can get.

'I do,' she disagrees. 'It wasn't a good phone call, was it?'

It seems clear she won't let this go, and, since not telling her would be hypocritical of me, I have no choice but to do so. 'No, it was not,' I say at last. 'It was my mother. I speak to her every night, but last night I missed her call and she wanted to know why.' I look down into Beatrix's blue gaze. 'I had to tell her that not only did I marry my father's widow, but that she's also expecting my child.'

CHAPTER SEVENTEEN

Beatrix

I LEAN INTO the warmth of Santiago's hard, powerful body. He's wearing only a pair of jeans, his magnificent chest bare, and it's difficult to think when he's half-naked like this. He's all hard muscle and velvety skin, with a sprinkling of crisp black hair, and it's incredibly distracting.

But this is important, so I force away my hunger for him.

I heard the hard note in his voice as I stepped out onto the terrace, saw the tension in his broad shoulders after he finished the call. His back was to me, but I knew from his posture that he was furious and so my first instinct was to go to him.

I didn't think about it. I didn't ask myself why it was important to touch him or to find out why he was so angry. I simply went to him and put my hand in the centre of his powerful back. And, when he turned around and saw me, pleasure flickered in his gaze, as if he was glad to find me there.

I'd decided yesterday not to press him about what kind of marriage we were going to have, accepting the physical pleasure he gave me last night instead, and glorying in it. But reality is hitting me now, because marrying him will have wider implications for us, and we really need to decide what we do about them.

What will the world think of him marrying his stepmother? What will they think when our child is born? Does it matter? Does he care? Do I? And have I given him too much of myself as it is?

I care about what I'm seeing in his face now, though, as he finishes telling me about the phone call. There's regret and anger, and beneath those a sharp pain that he probably thinks he's hiding, but he isn't. I can see it quite clearly.

'She didn't like that,' I say and I don't make it a question.

'No,' he says, more temper flickering in his eyes. 'She did not. She's very angry with me.'

His hands are cupping my rear, his fingertips pressing into my soft flesh and making my breath catch. I can't believe I want him again so soon after everything we did last night, but, as it turns out, my desire for him seems to have no end.

But again, I can't let sex distract me. This is too important.

I look up into his midnight eyes. 'I'm sorry,' I say, even though it feels like such a pointless comment.

'It's not your fault.' His voice is flat. 'She's been holding on to my father's betrayal of her for decades. And when he married you, that only reignited it for her. I knew she wouldn't be happy knowing we were together and expecting a child, but she had to find out the truth some time.'

'You don't like upsetting her,' I say, searching his face and seeing the truth.

His mouth tightens, his eyes shadowed. 'The addiction issues she had were compounded by me telling her the truth about my father all those years ago. Now I'm giving her yet another truth she doesn't want to hear. So no, I don't like upsetting her. I'm supposed to be caring for her, not hurting her.'

I can't stop staring up at him, because for the first time I catch a glimpse of the man who isn't just the furious, spurned stepson, the passionate lover and the cold, rational scientist. I see a human being upset about hurting someone he cares about.

He loves her just as he loved his father.

My focus shifts, his face blurring, then becoming clear again as my reality alters to fit this new truth. I know he's passionate—I experience his passion every night after all—but outside the bedroom everything else is kept under tight lock and key. Not now, though. His granite facade is cracking a little, and now I see a new facet of him. That of a loving son. A man who cares, and who cares deeply. It's a vulnerability, this caring, and he's showing it to me, and he probably doesn't even understand the significance of it. But I do. I know.

He loved his parents, but they didn't give him the same love in return, I'm sure of it. His father held a grudge for decades, reviling him at every opportunity, and perhaps his mother is the same. She's shooting the messenger and the messenger is always him.

My chest feels tight and hollow, aching with a feeling I can't quite place. It's not pity, it's something else, something deeper. It's not fair that his father was so angry with him for so long that Antonio took his anger to the grave with him, denying Santiago any chance of a reconciliation. And it's not fair that he's been taking care of his mother for so many years, only for her to give him back nothing but anger. It's not fair and I hate that it isn't.

'If it's not my fault, then it's not your fault, either,' I say, wanting to give him this at least. 'You didn't do any of this maliciously or to hurt her.'

'I knew it would, though,' he says, his black eyes full of even blacker shadows. 'She was making good progress and this will put her back.'

'You couldn't have hidden it,' I say. 'Like you said, she would have found out at some point.'

A muscle flicks in his jaw. 'Nothing is ever enough for her. Nothing I do was ever good enough for either of them.'

The words are a needle sliding under my skin, bringing hurt with it. Because I know what it's like to want to be good enough for someone. I tried to be good enough for that foster family who wanted to adopt me and Lisa. I tried so hard to be good, not throw any temper tantrums, and to obey their house rules, but in the end it wasn't enough. *I* wasn't enough.

'You're doing what you can for her.' I press my fingers against the warmth of his chest, wanting him to feel how much sympathy I have for him. 'And what you're doing is more than enough. More than a lot of people would do, actually. But her feelings aren't your responsibility, Santiago. Just as Antonio's weren't. They chose their own paths, and that's on them, not you.'

He stares down at me for a long moment, the shadows moving in his gaze. 'If I hadn't told them the truth, maybe they—'

'No,' I say fiercely, because he needs to understand this. 'You can't take responsibility for that, either. You were a child and you did what you thought was right. It's not on you that your parents chose to blame you instead of taking responsibility for themselves.'

Santiago's gaze bores into mine, a fierce heat glowing there all of a sudden. 'Why are you being so…kind to me,' he demands, 'after everything I did to you?'

'Because I know what it's like to feel as if you're not enough,' I tell him, spreading my fingers out on his skin. 'To question yourself. To try so hard for someone and it's still not enough, and you don't know what more you can do.'

For a moment, something springs between us. A current that for a change has nothing to do with chemistry or sex, and everything to do with mutual understanding. With knowing the experience the other person has had because you've been there too, and you feel the same way about it.

He doesn't speak, only bends his head and kisses me suddenly and fiercely. A kiss that tells me he recognises this moment too, and wants it just as much as I do.

But before I can deepen the kiss, he lifts his mouth from mine, then releases me. He steps back, the expression on his face unreadable. 'This means we'll need to talk about our marriage sooner rather than later,' he says. 'About all the things you mentioned yesterday. She'll be coming to live here at some point and it's best if we have all of that sorted out by then.'

His abrupt withdrawal feels almost painful, but I ignore it. If he doesn't want to talk more, then he doesn't want to talk. I'm his wife, but not in the romantic sense. We don't have that kind of relationship. Ours is practical, legal, and the fact that we're sleeping together is by the by.

So why are *you hurt, then?*

I decide to ignore that thought, too.

'Come,' he says, moving past me. 'Helene is preparing a tray. I'll bring it up to the bedroom and we can discuss everything there.'

He's gone hard, I can hear it in his voice. Perhaps he doesn't like that he was so vulnerable with me, and now wants to pretend that moment never happened.

I want to challenge him on his abrupt withdrawal, but I can't face it right now. I feel as if I've given too much of myself away to him already, and being hurt about this will only give him even more.

So, while he gets the tray, I go slowly back up to the bedroom. I need to armour myself again, protect myself, not let him get to me so intensely that every little thing he does takes on a deeper meaning. I'm not a teenage girl with her first crush. I'm an adult woman, pregnant with my first child, and, while he's my husband in a legal sense, he's nothing more than that. I can't let him be.

I move into the bedroom and go over to the bed, sitting down on it cross-legged to wait for him. What I need to think about is what I want out of this marriage. What sureties and certainties I can get for myself and for my child.

But what about him? What do you want from him?

I don't want anything from him, nothing at all. Yet as soon as I think that, it feels like a lie. It's almost as if I *do* want something from him, and not only pleasure. I want more of that understanding we shared downstairs, more of that look in his eyes when he turned around and found me standing behind him. More of that sense of…connection.

I've never had that before, not with anyone, but there's a reason for that. I never let my guard down, never let anyone in, because I don't want to be vulnerable to anyone. I don't have anyone to protect me, so I have to do it all myself.

But, as I told Santiago yesterday in the jewellery showroom, that makes for a lonely life, a bleak life. And I'm tired of being lonely. I'm tired of being afraid. I want a home and I want someone to share it with, I want to have a family, and the logical person to have that home and family with is Santiago.

I've told him more than I've ever told anyone about myself, and so far he's been nothing but understanding. But…do I let my guard down even more? And if

I do, where will it lead? Do I want the chance of a real relationship with this man I thought I hated?

I'm still thinking about it as he comes into the room, carrying a breakfast tray laden with all sorts of delicious things. Fresh croissants and jam and honey. A coffee pot. Glasses of freshly squeezed orange juice.

He puts the tray down on the mattress next to me, then sits on the end of the bed. 'Would you like honey on your croissant or jam?' he asks, picking up one of the flaky pastries.

'Jam, please,' I say.

He begins preparing the croissant for me, but I can tell from the look on his face that he's thinking about something else. And it's not something that's making him happy, not given the fury sparking and crackling off him even as his expression remains like granite.

'I can spread my own jam,' I offer, unsure of what to say.

'No,' he snaps. 'I'm perfectly capable of preparing breakfast for my wife.'

'Santiago,' I say, and before I know what I'm doing I reach across to him and put my hands over his. 'Stop.'

His sharp gaze comes to mine and I meet it head-on. 'Tell me what the issue is,' I say. 'You're still furious.'

'It's got nothing to do with you,' he retorts.

'It does if we're supposed to be having a discussion about our future.'

He pulls away from me, putting the torn croissant down on the tray. His expression has hardened, his gaze sharp, glittering points of obsidian. 'Perhaps a discussion is not the best idea now.' He looks at me, his attention roving over my body to my bare legs and back up again, lingering on the button of his shirt that I did up half-heartedly. 'Take off the shirt,' he orders. 'And lie down.'

I should do what he says. I don't want to disturb the connection we're starting to build between us, because it's fragile. But…regardless of where our marriage takes us, we're going to have to deal with each other for the rest of our lives because of our child. And I can't let that be a one-way street. I can't let his fury stop me from having the discussions we need to have for our baby's sake.

So I look him in the eye and lift my chin. 'No,' I say. 'If you're too angry to discuss this now, perhaps you should go away and deal with it. Then come back when you're ready to have a civilised conversation.'

CHAPTER EIGHTEEN

Santiago

HER SMALL, SLENDER FINGERS barely wrap around my hand, and yet it feels as if mine is enclosed in hers. Her skin is warm and her grip is firm. Her gaze as she looks at me is open, a deep midnight blue, and I want to throw myself into all that colour. Let it cool the heat of my fury. Let her touch calm me the way it calmed me downstairs.

Yet all I feel is furious.

That moment when Beatrix laid her palms on my chest, and looked up and saw me… Not the man I am, but the boy I used to be. The boy who once loved his parents, and who didn't understand why they didn't love him back. Why they never forgave him for one stupid thing he did, years and years ago. Why for one parent he was the devil, and for the other a source of attention that was never enough.

There was so much sympathy and understanding in her face in that moment, and all I wanted was to grab hold of her and never let her go, so I would always have her looking at me that way, giving me that sympathy and understanding that I never knew I was desperate for until now.

But a moment was all I could allow myself. She sees too deeply into me and I'm too hungry for that to let myself have it. The lines have the potential to become blurred. She's supposed to be my lover and legally my wife, and that's all, and I can't have her giving me sympathy or reassurance. I can't have myself wanting to share things with her, wanting to give her parts of myself, because I can't have this turning into something it's not. Something dangerous, something involving any kind of deeper emotions.

Something like love?

No. I can't let this be love. There's no surety in love, no safety. No certainty. Love is fickle and it can't be trusted, and it's never enough for some people, anyway. I don't want anything to do with it.

I stare back at her, forcing aside my anger, finding my usual rational, logical manner. 'I'm not angry,' I say, so determinedly neutral I'm sure I've betrayed myself. 'Let's discuss this marriage, then.'

'Now who's lying?' Her gaze is steady and sharp as a spear. 'I thought the truth was important to you.'

Yes, she sees me. She sees me even now, and she's making me feel like a hypocrite and a coward.

You're both of those things and you know it.

I ignore the thought, shoving it hard away, along with the helpless fury that I don't understand and don't want to. 'I'm not a liar, Beatrix,' I tell her coldly.

She shifts, sitting cross-legged on the mattress, and

looks back at me. Something's going on in that lovely head of hers, because I can see the way her blue gaze shifts and changes. God, I want to know what it is.

'I'm sorry, Santiago,' she says. 'I'm sorry for choosing Antonio. I wanted you, though. I wanted you badly. But I was afraid of the way I wanted you. I had a plan for my future, and you weren't part of that plan. But then you appeared that night of the fundraiser, and there was a part of me that knew I'd throw everything away just for a night with you. And I...couldn't even bring myself to go near you.'

Shock grabs me by the throat and it doesn't let go, and she doesn't stop. 'I haven't wanted to trust anyone for years,' she goes on. 'Because after that family didn't want me, I couldn't bear the thought of yet another rejection. Antonio was safe because he didn't require anything emotionally from me. He only wanted to have a pretty, young wife on his arm, and in return he would give me a home.' She pauses a moment, her gaze direct, open. 'I've never told anyone these things before. You're the first one.'

I don't know what to say to any of this. I don't even know why she told me. I'm a hard, difficult man, and I haven't given her any reason to trust me, and yet here she is, telling me all these things as if I have a right to them. She's taking off her armour, showing me the vulnerable parts of herself, trusting me with them, and I don't understand.

'Why?' I demand, my fury climbing, at her for being so stupid as to make herself vulnerable to me, and at myself for not knowing how to deal with it. 'Why tell me all of this?'

'Because you're the father of my child,' she says simply. 'And we're going to have to deal with each other in the future, regardless of whether or not we stay married.' She pauses and I can see that this is difficult for her, and that she doesn't want to say this next bit, but she does. 'And I'm lonely, Santiago. I want to let someone in. I want to trust someone. I want to share my life with someone, and I would like that someone to be you.'

There's nothing but truth in her eyes, and my chest tightens. I've had many lovers, women who don't want anything more than a couple of nights of passion, and I've never felt inclined to want more than that, either. I have few friends, most of whom are colleagues, other scientists in various parts of the world, and I only ever talk research with them. I have no one I confide in or talk to about anything else, because I'm difficult, and I've accepted that about myself.

You want what she's offering. You want it badly.

I want it, yes. But I can't offer the same in return. I can't and I won't, and that's just something she'll have to accept.

'I'm not an easy man,' I say after a moment, trying to find the language I need to explain. 'I'm diffi-cult. I have a short fuse, I'm impatient, I'm arrogant. I prefer facts to feelings, and I prefer reality over any kind of fantasy.'

The tension around her mouth relaxes. 'I mean, that

isn't news to me,' she says drily. 'Especially the arrogant part.'

'Beatrix,' I warn, because I can't treat this conversation lightly. 'Listen. You shouldn't trust me, and I don't know why you would. I haven't given you any reason to.'

But she only gives me one of her beautiful, aching smiles. 'Perhaps I don't need a reason,' she says. 'Perhaps I just wanted to make a leap of faith.'

'Beatrix—'

'Santiago,' she interrupts. 'You feel very deeply about a great many things, I can see that. And I think you'll feel very deeply about our child too. That's what I want to put my trust in. That depth of feeling.' She pauses. 'Also, who said you were difficult?'

That at least is an easy question to answer. 'It was made clear to me in no uncertain terms as I was growing up.'

'So…what? You just accepted it?'

I let out a breath and give her some more truth. 'I… tried to be different. Tried to be more…acceptable, shall we say? But nothing I did made any discernible difference. All I can be is myself, and if that's not good enough, then that's too bad, since it's all I can be.'

She is silent a long moment, studying me. Then she says, 'You don't need to be different. You're a complicated, fascinating man, and I like that a lot.'

Again there's a shifting in my chest, a tightness. She sees me and my many, many flaws and she thinks they're interesting. That *I'm* interesting. Yet as much as I want to believe her, I know the truth.

The evidence of caring that she's trusting in so much isn't there. Whatever care I once felt, it's gone now. The anger is merely the remains, and once that's burned away, nothing will be left.

Except this trust of hers is so fragile and delicate. It's a blown-glass rose she's giving me, the way she gave that white rose to a stranger, and it has to be handled with care, not smashed needlessly. I can't throw it back in her face. She sees in me the ghost of someone long gone, but I like that she sees it. It makes me feel as if I'm a better man than the man I've chosen to become. A less rigid, less difficult, kinder man.

I could try to be that man for her. I can do it. I've been trying all my life to be that man after all, and for her I could try a little harder.

So, I ignore my anger and slowly reach across the space between us, taking her hand and turning it over to find her palm. Then I bend and press a kiss there, like a promise. 'So,' I say, lifting my head and meeting her gaze, 'in that case, I want you to live here with me, sleep with me in my bed. My house is your house, and I will provide for you financially. This is your home. This is the place where you belong. You'll be my wife in every way.'

Her expression softens and there's a gleam in her eyes that looks like tears, though they're gone before I can say for sure. She smiles, though, and it's so beautiful I want to lock it away and keep it all to myself. 'I'd like that,' she says, her voice husky. 'I'd like that a lot. I'm even thinking that I'd also like to go back to school. Perhaps even to university. I'd like to have a career of my own doing something that I love, and not just out of necessity.'

I slide my fingers through hers, holding on to her hand. She's so lovely sitting there with her golden hair flowing down over her shoulders. The top few buttons of my shirt are undone and I can see the shadowed place between her luscious breasts. I want to undo the buttons and press my mouth there.

But she placed her trust in me, and I want to honour that. Sex would be an easy way to give her what she wants, but if I'm going to try to be the man she wants, I need to make a different decision. I need to have the conversation.

'A career?' I ask. 'What sort of things are you interested in?'

'I…don't really know.' Colour tinges her cheeks as if she's embarrassed. 'I wasn't very good at school. The foster home I was in at the time, the parents didn't care whether I did my homework or not, or whether I worked hard. So I didn't care either. I was just marking time until I was old enough to leave school and get out of the foster system.'

I've already thought she was strong and determined, and it's being reinforced for me now as I sit here, listening to her tell me about where she came from. And I find I don't like that no one cared about her or what she did. It feels like an insult. A travesty. She's beautiful and passionate, and stubborn. She's interesting, a fascinating subject that I keep discovering new things about, and it's wrong she has no one. So right then and there, despite knowing that it's dangerous to get any closer to her than I am already, I decide that she will have me.

I'm her husband. She's the mother of my child, therefore she's my responsibility, and, just as I would never walk away from my child, I won't walk away from her either. Not now.

'Well,' I say, 'you're not in the foster system now, and I care. If you want to go back to school or university, then I'll support you fully.' I pause, holding her gaze, letting her know I'm genuine in this. 'I want you to be happy, Bea.'

She tilts her head, looking at me. 'You do?'

'Yes,' I say. 'You deserve to be.'

Her colour deepens, her eyes shining as if I've given her a precious gift.

Careful.

It's true, this is venturing onto shaky ground. Her putting her trust in me is one thing, but her wanting something from me emotionally that I won't ever be able to give her is quite another. Because, while she is my responsibility, anything deeper will never be a part of this, not ever.

'But you have to know,' I go on, 'that I can't give you anything more than what I'm giving you now. Emotionally, I mean. Love, for example, can never be part of this marriage.'

For a moment something flickers in her eyes again, but it's gone before I can tell what it is. 'You'll love our child, though,' she says. 'Won't you?'

I can't help myself then, looking down at her stomach, hidden by the cotton of the shirt she's wearing, feeling that strong, powerful emotion tugging at me. An emotion I never wanted, yet I feel all the same.

'Yes,' I say, my voice a little rough. 'I will love our child.'

She pulls her hand from mine then, only to grab it again and draw it to her stomach, holding it there, my palm pressed to the hard, round shape beneath cotton and skin. Her eyes are suddenly alight, a smile playing around her mouth. 'I think he or she heard you,' she murmurs. 'Can you feel it?'

I do, a flutter against my palm. The kick of a tiny foot. And that powerful feeling gathers inside me in a roaring tide that threatens to undo me completely.

I might not love her, but this child I would die for.

CHAPTER NINETEEN

Beatrix

I'M STANDING IN the little room next to our bedroom that Santiago and I decided will be the nursery, trying to decide on what furniture we'll need. He's impatient to get the room ready, but we don't even know if we're having a boy or a girl yet, and, apart from that, my due date is still months away.

Since our conversation a couple of weeks ago, where I decided to give up all my vulnerabilities to him and to put my trust in him, he's been wonderful. He was wonderful then too, listening to what I said, then giving me a few of his own vulnerabilities. Telling me that he's not an easy man, that he's arrogant and prefers facts to feelings. That he's difficult.

I had to ask him about that and why he believed that about himself, and I wasn't surprised to hear that he was told that by his parents. But they were wrong about him, so, *so* wrong, and it angered me to hear it. Because I don't think he's difficult. I think he's a man who's armoured himself the way I armoured myself.

I did so with ice, while his armour is his formidable intellect and his rage. It protects him, yet it also hides the person he truly is, a man who worries about hurting his mother. Who tried to mend his relationship with his father. Who wants the best for his child. And who was hurt long ago, leaving him with no choice but to protect himself the best he could.

I didn't lie when I told him he was a man made of caring, because that's exactly what he is. The look on his face when I felt the baby kick, then put his hand on my stomach so he could feel it too, made everything female in me tighten. It was fierce, that look. Intense. Protective and possessive, and a deep part of me knew then that of course he would love his child. That look on his face was love.

But he won't love you, don't forget that.

No, I haven't forgotten. How could I? I haven't forgotten the sharp pain I felt the moment he said it, either. I don't know what that pain meant, and I don't want to know. It's enough for me that he loves our child and I'm not going to do anything to jeopardise that.

Anyway, he's helped me figure out what I want to study at university—science, oddly enough, which I wouldn't have thought about myself—and where and when. I'll begin the course after the baby is born, which will give me some time to prepare not only for the baby, but also for a new stage of life afterwards. And apart from anything else, my French needs to improve so I can actually attend and understand classes.

He's also released a low-key press statement about our relationship, and, while there was some initial fuss

and outrage, it gradually died down as the general public looked elsewhere for gossip.

His mother hasn't dealt with it, though, and she's
shut him out, refusing to answer his calls. It makes
me furious that she treats him this way, and I almost
want to intervene on his behalf, but I know that won't
help anything. In fact, it'll likely only make it worse.

He comes out of his study at night after every at-
tempted call, furious and tight-lipped, and I want to tell
him that maybe he should leave her be. Let her come
to some reckoning with it in her own time, because all
he's doing is hurting himself. But whenever I broach
the topic, he changes the subject. It's clear he doesn't
want to talk about it, so I don't push. I've been enjoying having someone to share things with too much
to disturb the delicate understanding we've come to.

As I frown at the huge wardrobe in the corner, trying to see if a changing table would fit there, I feel a
pair of strong, warm arms slide around my waist, drawing me up against a hot, hard male body.

'Are you making plans without me?' he murmurs
in my ear.

'No, of course not.' I smile and turn in his arms,
looking up into his dark eyes. 'I was only thinking of
where to put the changing table.'

He's usually so unreadable, but now one of his rare
smiles comes out and his face lights up. 'Oh, wait. I
have something to show you.' He releases me, and vanishes out of the door, only to return a few moments
later with a big rolled-up sheet of paper.

'Look,' he says, striding over to the guest bed and

unrolling the paper. 'I've done a plan for the room already.'

And he has. The plan has been drawn with great care and precision, the room absolutely to scale, with all the furniture thoughtfully placed. A crib here. A changing table there. A chest of drawers against one wall, and no wardrobe.

'I think we should put a door in from our room,' he says, gesturing to what he's drawn on the plan. 'So we can easily come and see to the baby in the middle of the night. And over here,' he points to another drawing, 'I think we should have a chair for you to sit in when you feed him or her.' He glances at me, his smile deepening. 'Or for myself when I do the feeding.' He looks thoughtful for a second then adds, 'Actually, if we get a really big chair, we can all sit in it together.'

And something gathers tight in my chest, something hot. A burning coal that just sits there, getting hotter and hotter, fuelled by his smile and the light in his dark eyes. Except they're not so dark now, they're brilliant, like a night full of stars, and I can't tear my gaze away.

We haven't talked in detail about how we're going to care for our child, but I know I don't want to get a nanny. I want to look after him or her myself, be a hands-on mother. I hadn't really thought of what kind of father he'd be at first, but now I know he loves the baby, I can see that love in his eyes now, burning so bright. He's taken time out of his busy day to draw this intricate and thoughtful plan, and he wants a door to our room for ease of access. And he's thought about me and my comfort, and the fact that he's even included himself in looking after the child…

This will be the family you always wanted for yourself.

Yes, it's true. And it won't just be me and my child, it will include him as well. He's included himself, and I can see it now, us with our baby sleeping in the next room. Him insisting it's his turn to do the night feed and letting me sleep, and then me doing the same for him. Then maybe both of us, sitting in the chair together, holding our child…

Our little family.

My eyes prickle with sharp tears, a lump sitting in my throat, and something is becoming clear to me. Something I should have realised long before now, perhaps even that day I arrived here, when I was sitting on the terrace and he told me that, even though my father didn't want me, *he* did.

Or maybe it was even before then, that night at the fundraiser when I saw him standing at the bar, and our eyes met. And I knew then that he'd be my ruin.

And he was. He is. Because I know what this hot glow in my chest is, and I know why I'm fighting tears. Why this feels like the end of the world.

I'm in love with him. I knew he was dangerous all those months ago, I knew he would end me, and he has. I'm ruined for anyone else, and I always will be, because he's the one I want. He's the *only* one I want.

He's frowning now, staring at me with some concern. He always picks up on my emotions. I can never hide anything from him. 'What's wrong, Bea?' He rises to his feet and comes over to where I'm standing, the concern in his gaze deepening. 'Are you okay?'

I don't want to tell him the truth, I don't. Because telling him I love him will break something. It'll break this fragile understanding we've arrived at, and I don't want to break it. It's good being in his bed every night. It's good having his arms around me. It's good talking for hours downstairs at the dinner table, long after the food has been eaten, simply talking about everything and nothing.

But I know that I can't keep this feeling to myself, that I have to tell him. He deserves to know. He's been very clear that he doesn't want love, but I think that's because his parents were both so selfish. They only had love for themselves, for their own pain and drama, and there was nothing left for him. They thought he was difficult, but he's not. He's been pouring all the love he had into them, and he got nothing back, and he blames himself. He thinks he's the problem, I know he does, but he's not. He was *never* the problem.

His feelings are protected and locked away to keep himself from being hurt. But he needs to know he doesn't have to do that with me. That he's enough just as he is, he never had to do anything else or be anything else. No matter how angry he was and sometimes still is, I love him all the same.

I love him.

'Yes,' I say, swallowing hard against the lump in my throat. 'I'm okay.'

He frowns and reaches to cup my cheek in his hand, his palm warm against my skin. 'So why are you crying?' His thumb brushes away an errant tear and I shiver… I can't help it.

This will break us, I know it. Or, at least, it'll break me, because he doesn't feel the same way. And by telling him, I'll have crossed a line that maybe I won't be able to cross back over.

But I've never loved anyone before, and I want to give him this. I want him to know that at least one person loves him for exactly who he is. Of course, he'll have to give me the truth in return, I know that, and it'll hurt. But I can't hide this truth from him. He's too smart not to see it, and anyway, I don't care about my pain. I'm used to it by now.

'I'm sorry, Santiago,' I say huskily. 'I know this isn't what you want to hear, but… I think…that I've…fallen in love with you.'

His gaze flares with shock, his hand dropping away from my cheek. 'What?' He sounds as if I've just told him someone's died.

I swallow hard yet again. 'I'm in love with you. I think I fell in love with you a couple of weeks ago, to be honest. But just seeing you with all these plans for our little family…' Another tear runs down my cheek, and I let it fall. 'It's everything I wanted for so many years.'

He's still staring at me and his face has gone white. His mouth has hardened into a line. 'I told you,' he says roughly. 'I told you that love would never be part of this.'

'I know,' I say. 'I know. And I don't expect anything—'

'You don't understand,' he interrupts, suddenly fierce. 'I don't want to hurt you, Beatrix. I don't. But you telling me this has put me in an impossible position.'

This time it's my turn to blink. 'What position?'

He lifts a restless hand to his hair, shoving his fingers through it distractedly. 'I have to tell you the truth and I won't lie. And it will hurt.' Anger flares in his eyes, familiar and hot. 'Fuck, all I ever do is hurt people.'

'No, no,' I say quickly, trying to deflect him from the path I can see he's heading down already. 'I didn't mean to put you in that position. I know you don't love me, Santiago, you were very clear about that.'

'No,' he says, his gaze holding mine, 'I don't. And I won't. You do understand that, don't you? It's not something that will grow with time or hit me out of the blue, or anything else. It's a conscious decision that I made years ago, and I'm not changing my mind just for you.'

He's furious, I can see that, and I knew he would be. It's the way he protects himself. So it's not unexpected, yet no matter how I told myself it wouldn't hurt, it does. It feels as if he's reached inside my chest, wrapped his long fingers around my heart and yanked it out, still bloody and beating.

But I draw myself up, because I'm not going to regret my decision or castigate myself for speaking up. And I'm certainly not going to apologise for loving him.

'I'm not asking you to,' I say as levelly as I can. 'I'm not asking you for anything you don't want to give. And I'm not going to push you or force you, or blackmail you emotionally. I'm not going to ask you for anything at all.'

That telltale muscle flicks in the side of his jaw. 'So why the fuck did you tell me?'

'Because I wanted you to know that you have someone who loves you. Someone who doesn't expect anything from you except to be the person you are. You don't have to take care of me, you don't have to take responsibility for me, and I'm certainly not going to be your duty.' I take a breath. 'I just love you.'

He's shaking his head, his eyes glittering with an emotion I don't recognise. 'You heard me, didn't you? That I'm never going to love you back.'

'I heard.'

'And what? That doesn't matter to you?'

I have to be truthful here, too. 'Yes, it does. But if you can't love me back, that's fine too.'

He's breathing faster now, fury in his eyes and all of it directed at me. 'How could you do this? What we had was good. Planning for the baby and—'

'We can still have that,' I interrupt. 'Nothing has to change.'

'Yes, it does,' he argues. 'Of course it does. How can we go on with this when you love me and I don't love you? How can you not be hurt by this?'

I lift my chin. 'My feelings are not your responsibility, Santiago. And I'm not apologising for them, either. If I tell you that nothing has to change, then it won't.'

He stares at me. 'And if I don't want you any more? What then?'

I know he's being deliberately blunt, deliberately honest, but it feels as if he's tearing strips from my soul. I didn't realise it would hurt like this. 'I don't know,' I say honestly. 'This was never going to be permanent anyway, right? That's what you told me. You made that very clear.'

He blinks, as if this is a shock to him. 'You can't stay here, Beatrix,' he says. 'We can't be here, not together. *I* can't be here.'

Another arrow hits me in the chest, another pain to add to all the rest, but all I do is nod. 'If you can't, then you can't. But you don't have to leave. This is your home. I'll go back to the hacienda.'

His dark eyes rove over me, the lines of his face hardening as he retreats from me once again, safe in his scientist persona. 'No,' he says curtly. 'I don't want you going back there. You will have the baby here as planned.'

'Okay,' I say simply, a certain resolution hardening inside me, too. I can't reach him with argument, I know that. I can't reach him with demands, either, since that's all his parents ever did, argue and demand. Going back to the hacienda won't work, since that's akin to leaving him, and I'm not going to leave him. He needs someone who'll stay, even if he's angry, even if he's cruel. He needs to know that someone loves him, despite all his thorns, and in spite of his fear, since that's slowly becoming apparent to me now.

He's afraid. He's afraid and he's pushing me away. But he won't be able to do that. I'm more stubborn than he is, and love has only intensified that stubbornness. I won't let him distance me, I won't.

'Okay?' he says, as if he's never heard the word before. 'That's all you have to say?'

'Yes,' I say, then turn for the door. 'If you're not going to be here for dinner, let me know so I can tell Helene.'

Then, without another word, I leave the room and close the door quietly behind me.

CHAPTER TWENTY

Santiago

I TURN FROM the whiteboard and pick up the eraser, angrily removing all trace of the equations on it. Again. I've done this so many times already in the past few days, and I'm tired of it. But my brain can't seem to make the connections I need it to, and I don't know why.

Tossing the eraser negligently down on the couch I've been sleeping on, I walk over to the windows and gaze out of them.

No, I know why I can't work. I'm too furious, both at Beatrix and at myself.

After she walked out of the guest bedroom, I tore up the plan I'd made for the nursery in a fit of rage and scattered the pieces on the floor. Then I left the house, because I couldn't stay in it, not with Beatrix being in such close proximity. She was too much of a temptation, and I'm too weak when it comes to her. I had to put some distance between us, because I couldn't bear to hurt yet another woman, no matter that she said that her feelings weren't my responsibility. I intended to stay at the office for as long as it took me to formulate some kind of idea about what to do next, yet I've been here for a few days now and I've yet to decide on anything.

One thing is becoming certain though: I have to go back to the house to pick up some papers and a research report that I left in the bedroom. I've got plenty of staff to do that for me, of course, but the report is confidential, and I don't trust anyone to get it without looking at it. Scientists are very jealous of their secrets, and I've had it happen a few times before where my research has been leaked to a competitor.

I turn from the view of Paris and call for a car. It's unfortunate to be returning to the house with Beatrix still there, but it can't be helped. I need the report, and with any luck she'll be out, so I won't run into her. Not for my sake, naturally—I'm mostly fine—but for hers. I don't want to cause her any unnecessary pain.

All the pain you caused her was unnecessary.

I ignore the thought, busying myself until the car comes. The trip home is spent on the phone, and when I get there I let myself in and go swiftly up the stairs to the bedroom.

Yet as I pass by the guest bedroom door, something tugs at me. A pain that's been there since I left, one I can't ignore, and so before I can stop myself I open the door and step into the room.

The first thing I see are the pieces of my plan scattered on the floor, and the sight of them makes the memory of her turning around and walking out return with painful clarity. Which then makes me furious all over again.

How could she do this to me? How could she fall in love with me when I specifically told her that love would *never* be a part of our marriage? And then to have the gall to tell me as if it was something *good*... something I *wanted* to hear.

I find myself pacing down one end of the room, before turning around and pacing back.

What did she expect me to do by telling me that? She knew what I would say. She knew that I had only the truth to give her, and so here I am again, hurting someone with the truth, the way I always hurt people with the truth. The way I always hurt people, full stop.

She said she wanted nothing from me, but I know she does. I could see the pain in her eyes when I told her that there was no way I could love her back, that I wouldn't.

If you don't care about her, then why are you so angry?

I reach the other end of the room, and turn around again, pacing back the other way.

I'm angry because I was enjoying our time together. I was enjoying helping her decide on her course of study, and holding her in my arms every night. Enjoying sitting at the dining table just talking, and knowing that she'd be here when I got home from a long night in the lab, and seeing her smile and knowing it was for me.

I liked it, and I didn't want it to end. But she spoiled everything, she broke everything.

She didn't break anything. She told you the truth, and you didn't like it.

Of course I didn't like it. We couldn't continue if she was in love with me. I'd only end up causing her pain, and I'm tired of causing people pain. The only solution is to cut love out, since love is the issue. It's a research problem with the simplest answer.

Except you can't do that with your child.

That's the one exception. I can't not love them or cut it out of any relationship I have with them. Biology prevents it, and that's something I've accepted. Just as I've accepted that loving my parents is part of biology…it's not something that can be helped.

But biology has nothing to do with my relationship to Beatrix, and so I chose to make love no part of it.

Except I can't stop seeing the tears in her eyes as she told me she loved me. Or the way her chin lifted as she told me that her feelings weren't my responsibility, that they were hers. The determination that filled her when she said it was fine if I didn't love her, that she didn't need me to love her back…

She *should* have someone to love her back, though. She deserves it. She should have the family she always wanted, with a husband who loves her the way she should be loved.

My heart beats faster as I reach the wall and then turn yet again, pacing another length of the room. Because the truth is I can't stand the idea of her finding another man, another husband. Of that glow in her eyes when she looks at me being there for someone else. Giving her smiles and her passion to someone else. Her fire and spark and wit to someone else. Her bravery to someone else…

This is an impossible problem and it has no solution.

Either I keep her with me, and hurt her terribly, or set her free to find someone else, and suffer the jealousy that will tear me apart.

There is another answer.

I stop dead in the middle of the room, my breathing coming faster and faster. There *is* another answer, another solution, and even though it's not something I ever wanted, I can't help thinking about it all the same.

I could love her back.

But love is painful and uncertain, and it can't be trusted. Love doesn't make anyone happy and it's never enough in the end. Certainly, it was never enough for either of my parents, yet…

She loves me. After everything I've done to her… reviled her, got her pregnant, dragged her here to Paris even though she didn't want to come, married her… After all of that…

I wanted you to know that you have someone who loves you. Someone who doesn't expect anything from you except to be the person you are…

Something takes hold of me, squeezing my ribs so tight I can barely breathe. I never knew what more I could do to get my father to forgive me, and I never knew what more I could do for my mother to make her happy. Who would want someone like that? Who could *love* someone like that?

Apparently Beatrix does. She loves the man I am, despite my very real and extensive flaws. I've never hidden them from her, not ever. She knows full well the extent of my arrogance and my pride, and my jealousy.

And she loves you anyway.

I look down at the floor, at the remains of my plan scattered there. A plan I spent hours over and loved every second of it, and ripped apart in a moment of rage. While she…calmly told me to let her know if I'd be around for dinner.

She should leave me, go and find someone else who isn't this jealous or difficult, someone easier than I am…

You don't want her to do that though.

My hands curl into fists at my sides. No, I don't want her to do that. I want her to stay. I want all her smiles and her laughter. I want her passion at night and the way she screams my name. I want her cool blue gaze to douse the fires of my anger. I want her to curl up in my arms with our child. I want her to tell me again and again that I'm enough.

I want her.

Then stop being such a fucking coward and choose her.

I stand there as it breaks over me in an icy wave of realisation. I'm afraid. I'm fucking afraid. I'm afraid of opening myself up. I'm afraid of not being enough for her, of *my* love not being enough. And knowing that makes this impossible problem an easy one to solve.

I could stop being afraid, and love this beautiful, passionate, special woman the way she deserves to be loved. I could give her what she's wanted this whole time, and I have the power. I have the power to give her everything she's always wanted, but only if I don't put my fear first. Only if I don't put *myself* first.

For a long moment I stand there, staring at the pieces of paper on the floor. I never wanted to be selfish like my parents, but I understand now that if I continue on this path I'll turn into a carbon copy of them. I can't do that, not with a child coming into this world. A child that deserves a better upbringing than I ever had. A child who deserves a better father than I had. And whose mother deserves more than a man who decides that loving her isn't as important as his own fear of being hurt.

I crouch on the floor, and slowly gather up the pieces of the plan I ripped up, then once I have them all I leave the guest bedroom and go downstairs to my study at the back of the house, my research report forgotten. Once I'm there I lay all the pieces of paper on my large oak desk and study them, my heart painful in my chest.

This room is what I wanted for my child, and it always included the mother of my child. I was thinking about her, and what she'd like, with every line I drew, and now she and what she'd like are stuck in my head.

There's a reason you can't stop thinking about her, why you were so angry with her for so long, why you were so afraid when she told you that she loved you.

I know. I can feel it inside me, the one truth I could never face, never even acknowledge. The truth that I was afraid of even looking at. The truth that I love her. That I've been in love with her all this time, from the moment I saw her. I told myself it was physical, just sex, merely chemicals and pheromones, nothing more, but it wasn't and never has been.

It's always been something deeper, something more. Something genuine. Something real.

I thought that I could keep my emotions separate from my rational thinking, that they were flaws. But they're not. They're part of my biology as much as my rational mind is, and I'm starting to realise something else, too.

Reality is made up of facts and love is one of those facts. Love is one of the fundamental truths of the universe, and, while it hurts, there's another side of it. Beatrix has shown me what that side is. Happiness. Joy. Laughter. Companionship. Acceptance. All the things I've never had from anyone else.

All the things that I know now I can only get from her.

The urge to find her is strong, but I need to do something first.

I sit at my desk, and slowly and carefully I piece my plan back together again.

CHAPTER TWENTY-ONE

Beatrix

I'M SITTING ON the window seat in the little sitting room, my stomach knotted, my throat aching. I thought I might at least start to feel better, as it's been a couple of days since Santiago walked out, but I don't. If anything I feel worse.

I'm trying to read a book right now, but my thoughts keep drifting, and I can't take in any of the words I'm reading. All I can think about is Santiago, wondering where he is and what he's doing, and what will happen when our baby is born.

I can't leave him, though, no matter how unpleasant he makes himself. I want him to know that love doesn't require him to do anything or to be anyone other than who he is. It doesn't make demands or ultimatums.

I do want him to love me, I can't deny that, and it hurts that he doesn't. But I'm not going to do to him what that family of so long ago did to me. I'm not going to get rid of him because he doesn't fit into my life, or because he's too rigid or demanding, or finds it difficult to express himself. I'm not going to get rid of him for *any* reason. I can't. He's too important, both to me and to our child, and besides, love isn't that petty.

I'm trying to read the same page of my book for the fourth time when suddenly the door to the sitting room bursts open, and Santiago comes in.

Every muscle in my body tightens in shock as I look up.

His hair is all over the place, as if he's run his fingers through it one too many times, and his black eyes are burning like hot coals. He's carrying the rolled-up piece of paper that he drew his plan on, but it looks as if it's been ripped apart then put back together with sticky tape.

I stare at him coolly, determined not to make a fuss. 'So, you're back. Will you be here for dinner tonight?'

'Fuck dinner,' he says roughly, going over to the coffee table and heedlessly pushing everything off it. Then he carefully lays down the piece of paper on the tabletop, before coming over to where I'm sitting. He pulls the book out of my grasp without a word, then takes my hand and draws me off the window seat, and over to the coffee table.

'Santiago,' I say breathlessly, 'what are you doing?'

'This,' he says and points at the plans. 'I want this.'

They've very definitely been torn apart, and then painstakingly pieced back together again. I stare at it for a moment and then look at him.

His eyes are burning brighter, the look on his face fierce in a way I don't recognise.

'You tore it up?' I ask, a little lump rising in my throat.

'Yes. I was angry.' He reaches for my hand and holds it in his, sliding his fingers through mine and gripping me tightly. 'I was angry with you for telling me what you did. For breaking what we had.'

My throat is constricted, and I want to draw my hand away, but his grip on me only tightens even further. 'I know you were,' I say. 'But I'm not sorry and I don't take it back.'

'I don't want you to be sorry,' he says, focusing on me with the kind of sharp intensity that takes my breath away. 'I don't want you to take it back. In fact, what I want is to keep hearing it from you every day of my life for the rest of my life. I want you to love me, Beatrix. I want all of your love, and I want it forever. And…' he pauses a moment, looking into my eyes '…I want to love you back.'

Everything in me freezes, the breath catching in my throat. 'But you said you didn't want—'

'I know I did.' Slowly, he pulls me in closer and closer. 'But I was wrong. The truth wasn't that I didn't love you. The truth was that I did. I do. I just didn't want to acknowledge it. All my life my love has never been enough for my father or my mother. They were always too wrapped up in their own emotions to consider mine, and I thought love was the issue. *My* love. But…' he pulls me even closer, his other hand sliding to the small of my back and pressing there, so I'm up against his hard, hot body. '…I think in the end love wasn't the problem. Love was the solution.'

I'm trembling all over now, barely able to take in what he's saying, because he can't be saying he loves me, can he? Or maybe only that he wants to?

'I don't understand,' I say shakily. 'What do you—'

'I love you, Beatrix,' he interrupts, even more fierce now. 'You showed me what love could be, and I didn't understand until just now. All I ever saw were the downsides, only the lies and the pain. I never saw anything good in it. But there's good in it. There's your smile and your bravery, and your stubbornness. There's your passion and your wit, and your care. You showed me what it could be and I want… I want to try and give you the same in return.'

My throat has closed up completely, my heart inflating behind my ribs like a balloon, filling up with all the love in my being. All the love I have for him. 'You don't have to try, you idiot,' I manage to force out, my voice husky. 'What you're doing already is enough, as I keep telling you.' I pull my hand from his, and raise both of mine to his beautiful face, cupping it between my palms. 'I love you, Santiago, and not in spite of your flaws. I love all of you, even the parts of yourself you don't like. Because they make up who you are, and without them you wouldn't be you.'

His eyes glow, like dark stars at midnight, and I go up on my toes and press a kiss to his hard, beautiful mouth.

'I love that plan, too,' I whisper. 'Even in pieces.'

He smiles and it's like the sun coming out. 'I can draw it again.'

But I shake my head. 'No, I like that you put it back

together. It feels as if that's what you did with my heart. You broke it, then put it back together again.'

His arms come around me, pulling me in close. 'I will never break it again, pretty Bea. Never again.'

And he never did.

Even now, he keeps it as a treasure, as I do with his.

We're binary stars, he often tells me, orbiting each other forever. Except I disagree about one thing. Binary stars never touch, and we do. A lot.

But the forever part is true.

EPILOGUE

Santiago

WE RETURNED TO Spain six months after our little Mia was born. Beatrix wanted to bring her up in Spain, at the Veracruz estate, and I agreed. I was apprehensive at first, since being at the hacienda brought back some bad memories, but I soon realised that my fears were groundless. With Beatrix and Mia, it felt new and different, and after we refurbished the whole place it began to feel like home.

I had a long talk with my mother, telling her that she had to accept the situation with Beatrix and that both she and I would like her to have a relationship with her granddaughter. After that it was like a switch had flipped. She started doing much better, and at last she was well enough to come home, choosing to live in my house in Paris. She's gradually coming around to the idea of Beatrix being my wife. but she very much loves her little granddaughter, and has let us know that she'll be coming to Spain for a visit at Christmas.

Now I'm lying in our bed in the hacienda, waiting for my wife to join me after putting Mia down to sleep. I'm hungry for her as I always am…that hasn't changed. She's a conundrum that is never solved, a puzzle that continues to fascinate the more I learn about her.

I don't know what kind of life we could have had if my father hadn't married her, but if he hadn't Mia wouldn't have been born and I wouldn't change that for the world. I wouldn't change how Beatrix came to me either.

She steps into the bedroom, still wearing a robe, and I raise a brow. 'It's appalling you should come to my bed still fully dressed,' I say.

'I'm not fully dressed. I'm wearing a robe.'

'As I said. Fully dressed.'

She laughs, and pulls something out of the pocket of said robe, before coming down onto the bed next to me. Then she lifts her hand and I see she's holding a long plastic stick. There are two pink lines in the window.

My heart catches. 'Bea,' I murmur. 'Oh, Bea.'

Her eyes are a lake in full sunlight and she laughs again as I pull her hard against me, and kiss her senseless.

I was right to think that love was a fundamental truth.

It is. And it's endless, bottomless. You can never have too much and it never runs out. It's always there, a well that never runs dry.

* * * * *

Did Heir with My Enemy *leave you enthralled?*
Then don't miss Jackie Ashenden's
other dramatic stories!

Newlywed Enemies
King, Enemy, Husband
Christmas Eve Ultimatum
His Heir of Revenge
His Forced Sicilian Bride

Available now!

Get up to 4 Free Books!

We'll send you 2 free books from each series you try
PLUS a free Mystery Gift.

Both the **Harlequin Presents** and **Harlequin Medical Romance** series feature exciting stories of passion and drama.

YES! Please send me 2 FREE novels from Harlequin Presents or Harlequin Medical Romance and my FREE gift (gift is worth about $10 retail). I may cancel anytime by emailing ReaderServiceInfo@Harlequin.com or by calling 1-800-873-8635. If I don't cancel, I will receive 6 brand-new larger-print novels every month and be billed just $7.19 each in the U.S., or $7.99 each in Canada, or 4 brand-new Harlequin Medical Romance Larger-Print books every month and be billed just $7.19 each in the U.S. or $7.99 each in Canada. That's a savings of 20% off the cover price! It's quite a bargain! Shipping and handling is just 75¢ per book in the U.S. and $1.75 per book in Canada.* I understand that accepting the free books and gift places me under no obligation to buy anything—they are mine to keep for free no matter what I decide.

Choose one:

☐ **Harlequin Presents Larger-Print**
(176/376 BPA G3CD)

☐ **Harlequin Medical Romance**
(171/371 BPA G3CD)

☐ **Or Try Both!**
(176/376 & 171/371 BPA G3CE)

Name (please print)

Address   Apt. #

City   State/Province   Zip/Postal Code

Email: Please check this box ☐ if you would like to receive newsletters and promotional emails from Harlequin Enterprises ULC and its affiliates. You can unsubscribe anytime.

Mail to the **Harlequin Reader Service:**
IN U.S.A.: P.O. Box 1341, Buffalo, NY 14240-8531
IN CANADA: P.O. Box 603, Fort Erie, Ontario L2A 5X3

Want to explore our other series or interested in ebooks? Visit www.ReaderService.com or call 1-800-873-8635.

HPHM2603